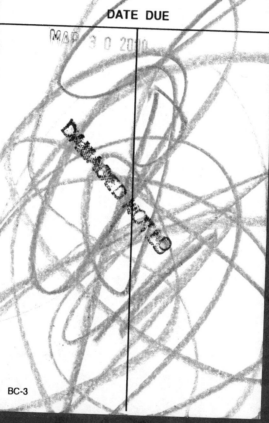

Let My People Go

Bible Stories told by a freeman of color to his daughter,
Charlotte, in Charleston, South Carolina, 1806–16

by PATRICIA *and* FREDRICK McKISSACK

illustrated by JAMES E. RANSOME

An Anne Schwartz Book
Atheneum Books for Young Readers

To our children: Fred, Jr. and Lisa; John, Michelle, and Baby; Robert; and
the children of Olive Chapel A.M.E Church
—P. and F. M.

To Lesa, Jaime, Maya, and Malcolm
—J. R.

ACKNOWLEDGMENTS

Four years ago our editor, Anne Schwartz, suggested that we write a Bible storybook. Conceptualizing, researching, writing, revising, and finally realizing the completion of this book is a triumph of the heart. It took a lot of patience and persistence on the part of a lot of people to make it all happen. Although it is impossible to name all of those who helped us along the way, we'd like to thank a few special people, such as Rabbi Louis Frishman of Temple Beth El, Spring Valley, New York; Dr. W. Marvin Dulaney of the Avery Research Center, Charleston, South Carolina; the Reverend Brenda Hayes, Pastor of Olive Chapel African Methodist Episcopal Church, Kirkwood, Missouri; the Reverend Mickey Hassler, West Side Baptist Church, St. Louis, Missouri; St. Louis Public Library Research staff; Joan Stevenson, Henrietta Smith, John McKissack, Sarah Knight, James Ransome, and a very special thanks to Anne Schwartz, whose confidence in us and enthusiasm for this project never wavered.
—P. and F. M.

I would like to thank my support system that fueled James Ransome, the person and the illustrator. First, my wife, Lesa, I love you and thanks for so many things, but most of all for giving me courage. My children, Jaime, Maya, and Malcolm, thanks for keeping me real and making me laugh. My dog, Clinton, thanks for the quiet times, three times a day. Jerry Pinkney, "The Man," thanks for everything. Love ya. Tom Feelings, thanks for the long talks. I hope they never stop. They make me fly. Patricia and Fredrick McKissack, thank you for creating this wonderful text. I wish I could have painted a picture for every paragraph. Anne Schwartz, my editor, thanks for believing in my work. Shelley Fogelman, my agent, thanks for your wisdom. And last but not least, thanks to Jesus for the example He set that I strive to follow. And to His Father, My Lord, for all His blessings. —J. R.

Atheneum Books for Young Readers
An imprint of Simon & Schuster Children's Publishing Division
1230 Avenue of the Americas
New York, New York 10020

Book design by Edward Miller and Ann Bobco
The text of this book is set in Centaur.
The illustrations are rendered in oil paint.
First Edition
Printed in the United States of America
10 9 8 7 6 5 4 3 2 1
Library of Congress Cataloging-in-Publication Data
McKissack, Pat, 1944–
Let my people go : Bible stories told by a freeman of color to his
daughter, Charlotte, in Charleston, South Carolina, 1806–16 / by
Patricia and Fredrick McKissack ; illustrated by James Ransome.
—1st ed.
p. cm.
"An Anne Schwartz book."
Includes biographical references.
Summary: The daughter of a free black man who worked as a black-
smith in Charleston, South Carolina, in the early 1800s recalls the
stories from the Bible that her father shared with her, relating them
to the experiences of African Americans.
ISBN 0-689-80856-9
1. Afro-Americans—Juvenile fiction. [1. Afro-Americans—Fiction.
2. Slavery—Fiction. 3. Fathers and daughters—Fiction. 4. Bible
stories—O.T.] I. McKissack, Fredrick. II. Ransome, James, ill. III.
Title.
PZ7.M478693Le 1998
[Fic]—dc21 97-19983
FIRST EDITION

Contents

AUTHORS' NOTE

During the segregated 1950s, when we were public school students, African American heroes weren't included in our curricula or featured in our history books. Fortunately, we had a Sunday school teacher who was a masterful storyteller, who mesmerized us with narrations about ancient biblical characters and African American historical figures simultaneously. First, he had us imagine what it would be like to wait in the dark den alongside brave Daniel as he faced down the lions with his unyielding faith. Then, in a blink, we were standing onstage with abolitionist Frederick Douglass as he courageously confronted hostile pro-slavery audiences. In this compelling way, we were shown the parallels between two heroic people from different cultures and distant time periods. The Bible came alive for us; it was the source of great ideas that we could use in looking for solutions to the social injustices of our own time.

We decided to use that same approach in this book.

The Bible is, among many things, the religious account of the Hebrew people and their relationship with God. The stories are timeless treasures, universally read and honored, but no group embraced the Hebrew heroes of old more than African Americans during slavery times. Moses, for example, was second only to Jesus in the love and respect he commanded in slave quarters. The promise of freedom as it was described in the Book of Exodus gave another oppressed people a reason to hope and to keep on, in spite of their suffering. This is especially evident in the spirituals that slaves created. When they lifted their voices and cried out, "Tell ol' Pharaoh to let my people go," they were singing about their faith that one day God would send a deliverer to free them also.

Since the Bible was such an important part of our slave ancestors' lives, we targeted the early nineteenth century slave period as our historical backdrop. We chose to set the book in Charleston, South Carolina, a city that fascinated us because, as a Southern port, it played a major role in the American slave trade *and* was home to a large community of free blacks. We've retold twelve Old Testament favorites in the distinctive voice of a fictionalized free black abolitionist, Price Jefferies.

Jefferies is loosely based on an actual free black of Charleston, Denmark Vesey, an African captive who was sold into slavery and served many years aboard a merchant ship. Upon winning a seamen's lottery in 1800, he bought his freedom and hung out his shingle as a craftsman. But here the similarities between the two men end. Vesey organized a slave rebellion in 1822 and was hanged when the plot failed; Price Jefferies is a family man whose rebellion takes a quieter form. Still, he is equally committed to the abolition of slavery and willing to put his life in jeopardy to defend his beliefs.

The narrator of the book is Price Jefferies' daughter, Charlotte Jefferies Coleman, who was modeled after Frances Ellen Watkins Harper, an outspoken nineteenth century abolitionist, feminist, and poet. Writing as an adult, Charlotte recalls incidents from her young life that led her father to tell her Bible stories. Although these vignettes are specific to Charlotte's own life, we've tried to make them universal in the subjects and themes they explore.

A particular challenge was to create historically accurate voices for Charlotte and Price. We've given Charlotte speech that is characteristically formal, representative of a well-educated black woman of the nineteenth century. However, in conversations she recalls from her childhood, her young voice echoes that of her parents. Price, while a man of means, a fine craftsman, and literate, has not been formally educated. So his storytelling voice slips into the more comfortable dialect of the deep South. He doesn't use the Gullah that might be associated with South Carolina's Sea Island black culture, though he may occasionally season his retellings with a Gullah phrase, such as *day clean*, which means *dawn*. We imagined that Price, like Vesey, learned English while onboard ship, and his speech was more like those slaves whose masters were lower-class English-speaking sailors.

The genesis of this project began with a childhood memory, a "mustard seed" idea that started us on a journey of discovery and renewal. What follows is the result of years of growth through research and study, and months of writing and revision. Our hope is that this book will be like a lighthouse that can guide young readers through good times and bad; that it will show others that the Bible is a wonderful tool to help meet the challenges of daily life. The ideas these ancient stories hold are not for one people, at one time, in one place. They are for all of us, for all times, everywhere.

Patricia and Fredrick McKissack
Chesterfield, Missouri

ILLUSTRATOR'S NOTE

In our home in the small town in North Carolina where I grew up, the Bible was the only book we owned aside from a set of encyclopedias. I was raised by my grandmother, Ruby G. Ransome, a deeply religious woman who attended church and Sunday school regularly. Jesus, the Baptist Church, and the Bible were her foundation.

When I was eight or so, Grandma Ruby, who had only a first-grade education, began asking me to read the Bible to her. And as I read, the illustrations—filled with figures in dramatic poses wearing flowing garments and surrounded by beautiful landscapes or elaborately detailed architecture—sparked my imagination. Because art wasn't offered in the rural school I attended, I was teaching myself how to draw. These images became some of the first I tried to imitate.

The Bible illustrations continued to influence me as I matured as an artist. (For example, my interest in painting the figure began with those paintings.) Although my earlier books are not as grand in scale, I knew that in *Let My People Go* I would return in look and feeling to what had originally inspired me to paint.

But there would be one major difference. The people would resemble those from the region of North Egypt and what we now know as Israel, Lebanon, Syria, Iraq, Jordan, Ethiopia, and north of Saudi Arabia—where most of the Old Testament stories took place. I would draw people with brown and olive complexions, Semites. I felt compelled to dispel the myth created by the European representations of Bible characters, so fixed in the minds of most of us. I felt it was time to start educating our children about the true images of the people who gave the world the concept of one God and three religions: Judaism, Christianity, and Islam.

The reader will notice two painting styles. My illustrations of Price Jefferies and his daughter are done in a limited palette—mostly browns and white with one strong color. The Bible paintings, like those that moved me as a child, are more colorful, and full of romantic gestures and elaborate architecture.

Rendering these paintings has been a labor of pure love. It has reconnected me to those times when my grandmother and I would sit with the Bible between us, sharing the stories of a strong and resilient people not unlike ourselves.

James E. Ransome
Poughkeepsie, New York

*O*h, God! we thank thee, that thou didst condescend to listen to the cries of Africa's wretched sons; and that thou didst interfere in their behalf. At thy call humanity sprang forth, and espoused the cause of the oppressed: one hand she employed in drawing from their vitals the deadly arrows of injustice; and the other in holding a shield to defend them from fresh assaults: and at that illustrious moment, when the sons of '76 pronounced these United States free and independent; when the spirit of patriotism erected a temple sacred to liberty; when the inspired voice of Americans first uttered those noble sentiments, "We hold these truths to be self-evident, that all men are created equal, that they are endowed by their Creator with certain unalienable Rights; that among these are Life, Liberty, and the pursuit of Happiness"; and when the bleeding African, lifting his fetters, exclaimed, "am I not a man and a brother"; then with redoubled efforts, the angel of humanity strove to restore to the African race the inherent rights of man.

Peter Williams, Jr.
"A Prayer for Africa's Children," 1808

Charlotte's Introduction

Today the Thirteenth Amendment to the United States Constitution was ratified, and slavery is abolished in our land forever. Oh, I am happy, happy beyond belief that this day has come at last!

The hour is late. I've just now finished the final issue of *The Trumpet*, the abolitionist journal I have managed and edited for over thirty years. Yet I'm too excited to think of rest or sleep. I want to cling to the joy of the moment and bask in the warmth of victory.

My only regret is that my dear father is not here to rejoice with me. It was Papa who encouraged me to use my writing talents to further the cause of the abolitionists; Papa who said, "To whom God has given much, much is required."

My father was the first abolitionist I ever knew—although he certainly would have preferred to be remembered simply as a good man. Unlike other blacks who lived under the shadow of slavery at the turn of the century, he was a freeman of color; my mother and I were free too.

By trade, Papa was a blacksmith, respected for his craftsmanship. But he'd known the cruelty of slavery, having been captured as a boy in West Africa and forced to serve onboard a slave ship. Papa had seen firsthand the horrors that African captives endured as they were transported from the breeding plantations in the Caribbean Islands to ports in Brazil, New Orleans, and Charleston. He'd watched as human beings were auctioned off as chattel, no different from cattle or horses.

In 1793, when Papa had less than twenty years, he won a seamen's lottery. I remember him telling me many times how the other sailors often used their food allowance to buy a chance to win several thousand dollars. Papa never had, but one day he took a chance. To everybody's surprise, he won the pot, then used the money to buy his freedom.

Turning his back to the sea, Papa settled in Charleston. He convinced the Reverend Silas Jefferies, a freeman of color and a blacksmith, to take him on as an apprentice. It was his surname that Papa took as his own. From him Papa learned to be an artisan and a man of faith. He studied the Bible and its wonderful cast of characters, whose stories contain messages of faith, hope, love and, above all, justice for a downtrodden people. Papa loved to tell me how the Reverend Jefferies, armed with the mighty sting of truth, would remind slaveowners of God's message to Pharaoh: "Let my people go!"

Papa passed this wisdom he had learned on to me. I grew up believing that, because slavery was *wrong*, God would not abide it—no matter how slaveholders tried to defend it.

It was clear to me from my earliest years that Papa was a man of great spiritual integrity. Naturally, I saw him through a daughter's eyes—a giant of a man, when actually he was well under six feet tall. When he picked me up, I felt only the strength of his hands, not the calluses. When he laughed, I saw only the sparkle in his eyes, not the scars that peppered his face, caused by flying sparks from the hot anvil. I never realized how long and hard Papa worked. I knew only that I loved being near him, listening to him tell the stories that had shaped his beliefs.

My favorite spot was on top of the woodpile, where I could listen to the rhythm of his hammer as he crafted a magnificent iron gate for a wealthy rice planter or repaired the handle of an ordinary skillet, while at the same time he skillfully hammered out a Bible story of equal beauty and usefulness.

I later learned that Bible stories worked well within the oral tradition of the West African griots of Papa's homeland because they could be used to entertain as well as teach. I can still hear his deep voice telling a gathering about the creation of the world, Noah and the Flood, Moses standing at the Red Sea, the lowly birth of a baby born in a Bethlehem stable, and the work of the Twelve Apostles. He talked about Bible characters as if they were personal friends, even though they were great Hebrew heroes who lived long ago and far, far away from Charleston, South Carolina. Still, their trials and tribulations, their triumphs and blessings, were as familiar to me as a fresh drink of water. I understood their problems and celebrated their victories. For centuries these stories have helped oppressed people find courage and strength, endure hardships, fight against incredible odds, and triumph over tyranny.

Papa may have died before slavery ended, but his ideas live on in the Bible stories he cherished. He understood that the great stories of the Hebrew children whom God loved were our stories, too. He knew that God's same love would deliver us in our time of need, and one glorious day, the sufferings of so many among us would ease. The words "Let my people go!" would be heard at last.

The courage and commitment I learned from my father have sustained me during our long struggle for freedom. Now it is my turn to pass Papa's legacy on, to tell the old, old stories to you who face more troubled waters in your fight for justice and equality.

Come, join me as I take you back to Charleston, South Carolina, to my father's forge in the early 1800s. Sit with me on the woodpile as he tells a tale of faith, hope, or love. Let his simple words cool you in the heat of the day, or warm you on a cold, rainy night. Listen to the clanking of his hammer and the richness of his voice as he retells each story in the bold and rhythmic voice that was uniquely his own.

Charlotte Jefferies Coleman
Philadelphia
December 1865

Something Wonderful Out of Nothing

THE CREATION

Genesis 1: 1–31

Genesis 2: 1–7; 22

One summer night in 1806 Papa and I were walking home from visiting a friend. The sun had set, but it was not yet dark. A generous breeze stirred the air and made the heat more agreeable. We had not walked far when we met a constable. I was frightened because they were usually rough-edged men with few, if any, manners. I held close to Papa.

As I'd feared, the constable stopped us. "Hey you, there," he said gruffly. "Don't you belong to Mr. Sam Riley?"

I was just a sliver of a girl, with six years at the time, but I remember Papa pulling his shoulders back. "I am Price Jefferies, a blacksmith by trade," he said proudly. "This, my daughter, Charlotte. We be free people."

The constable examined our papers, then waved us on with a disgusted scowl.

I knew that Mr. Sam Riley was one of the wealthiest planters in Charleston, rich enough to own whatever he had a mind to have. Just how much *did* he own? I wondered.

By the time we got back to our house, the moon had risen on a sky of blue velvet. I watched it float higher and higher into the sky. I was enjoying the night so much, I felt a bit guilty, as though I were stealing a joy that didn't belong to me. Suddenly I blurted out my concern to Papa. "Do Mr. Sam Riley own the moon?" I asked.

Papa looked up in surprise. His big shoulders shook as a wave of laughter burst from his chest. "Sam Riley may own just 'bout everything else in Charleston Town, but no, Dumplin', the moon don't b'long to him. Neither do the sun, the wind, nor one tiny star." He sat me on top of the woodpile. I could feel a story coming, and I wasn't wrong. "Let me tell you 'bout how it was in the beginning," Papa said, "when there come something wonderful out of nothing."

Imagine this, if you can. Nothing. Nothing at all. That's the way it was in the beginning. Nothing, 'cept God the Almighty. How long? I can't rightly say for how long, 'cause there wasn't no time yet. But it's safe to say that by and by, God took a notion to make something wonderful out of nothing.

At the beginning the Almighty made the heavens and then the Earth. Understand now, neither one looked much like they do today. The earth had no rhyme or reason; it was cold, no sound, no life. The heavens were wrapped in a forever darkness, darker than a hundred moonless nights. But God's great, loving spirit was in the middle of it all, moving gentlelike over the watery mist, covering it up in a blanket of quiet love. There, the Creator took time to study on what to do with the heavens and the earth.

When it was right and good, God called out in a loud, clear voice, "Let there be light." And quick like the blink of an eye, the light came into being. God saw its brilliance and called it Day. God saw the beauty of the darkness and called it Night. Night came. Morning followed. That set the order of the very first day and all the days that have followed ever since.

Come back with me now to the second day. God spoke once more and again, saying, "Let there be a firmament in the midst of the waters, and let it divide the waters from the waters." Everything that heard God's voice obeyed. The sky snapped into being, and some of the waters moved up above it, and some of the waters moved down below it. God called the firmament Heaven.

On the third day, God called forth the dry land and told the waters to collect in one place. The echo of those mighty commands reached down to the foundation of the earth and heaved up mountains and scooped out the valleys, the lowlands, and marshes. The waters rushed to form the great salty seas and the swift-running rivers. And every spring, every creek, and every pond filled up with clean, fresh water.

The sky snapped into being

Then with the wave of the Master's hand, pine forests and shady woods dressed ol' Mother Earth in a garment of green. Grasses and herbs, trees, vines, and bushes bloomed and brought forth all manner of colorful flowers and fruits.

Imagine planting turnips and up come okra. Wouldn't that be a funny sight, seeing lilacs blooming on rosebushes, or onions growing on a grapevine? But not to worry, the Creator took care of that by commanding the seed of every plant to bring forth another plant just like itself, every time. That's the way it was in the beginning and that's the way it is now.

The Creator's 'tention turned toward the heavens on the fourth day. First thing, God molded the sun and placed it in the sky to rule the days. Sister Sun's been risin' in the east and settin' in the west without fail, season following season. Sister Moon, a smaller light, was created to rule over the night sky. Both lights help us to know night from day, and how to count the passing of time. God saw all of this beauty and say, "It is good."

The fifth day found God creating the birds and every flying creature, all free to swoop and soar through the air on new wings. God then created fishes and all creatures that swim in the waters from the minnow to the whale. And God commanded them to multiply and to become many upon the earth, and everything obeyed. The night came. Day followed.

God started early on the sixth day, creating every animal that creeps, crawls, slithers, or slides. Critters of all sizes and shapes skittered and scattered, lumbered and blubbered their way 'cross the land. Big ones and little ones roamed the grasslands in herds and took to the hills, the forest, and lowlands. What a sight to behold, the earth teeming with so much life.

The Good Book don't say so, but I imagine the Great God Almighty stood on the crest of the highest mountain and looked over all creation. Everything was as it was s'posed to be. The sun, the moon, the stars occupied the heavens. The earth was alive with plants and animals. God saw it all and say, "It is good." But for some reason the Creator wasn't altogether satisfied. Something was a-missing.

Then an idea came. It was small at first, but it grew and grew until at last, the Lord God just shouted out with pure excitement, "Let us make man!" Straightaway man and woman were created in the image of their Creator, and yes, that ended the sixth day.

Seeing all that had been done, God smiled and say, "It is very good." On the seventh day, our Lord rested.

Nobody can make a slave of the moon, the sun, the stars, or any part of what God created, no matter how rich they may be. God made something wonderful out of nothing. What human being can do that?

Making Choices

THE FALL and CAIN AND ABEL

Genesis 2: 16–17

Genesis 3: 1–24

Genesis 4: 1–16

On the first Monday of the month Papa had business at the Exchange Building at the corner of East Bay and Broad Streets. For years he had never taken me because slave auctions were held on the north side of the building. Papa didn't want me to see a slave auction, but I felt a strange curiosity about it and begged him to take me. The year I turned ten, he allowed me to go with him.

When we arrived, two ships had weighed anchor and were getting ready to unload their cargo. They had such happy-sounding names, the *Amity* and the *Felicity.* But nobody was fooled: I knew the horrible truth of what filled the belly of these monstrous vessels.

As the seamen began unloading the fresh shipment of African captives, I realized most of them were not much older than me. Chained foot to foot and naked to the waist, they were led to a filthy holding pen where they waited to be sold. Some marched with their heads squared on their shoulders, showing no signs of weakness before their captors. Others cringed and cowered in submission. A few of them looked sick, even though they had survived the ten-day quarantine period on Sullivan's Island, where they'd been checked for diseases. One poor girl looked completely insane, driven mad by what she had been through.

I squeezed Papa's hand and shut my eyes, for I had seen enough. After pleading to come, now all I wanted to do was go home.

Papa quickly finished his business. We were about to leave when all at once, there was a commotion over by the holding pen. One captive's cry rang out above the din. Papa recognized some of the words as Mende, the language he had spoken when he was a boy in Africa. Guiding me along with him, he quickly pushed his way through the crowd.

Papa started to respond, but he was pulled aside by a bearded sailor who cursed at him, saying, "You knows the rules. No Guinea-talk."

The captive was brought up for bid. His frail body began to shake uncontrollably. Rivers of sweat meandered down his face and body. It made my stomach churn to see another human being suffering so.

"That slave looks like he's got the ship sickness," I heard one buyer say to another, fear creeping into his face.

"He must not have been spotted over on the island," said the other.

"No telling what he's got!"

The captive moaned, and I looked into his pleading eyes. "Can't we help?" I asked Papa.

Immediately he called out, "Five dollars."

Papa's bid caused a stir. "That's Price Jefferies, the blacksmith," a woman shouted angrily. "He's known for buying slaves, then freeing them."

"No need to worry. That one aine worth two dead flies," somebody answered.

My eyes never left the captive who had begun bouncing from foot to foot, up and down, in a strange sort of dance. Then I realized it was a death dance. The poor boy was dying. *Don't give up,* I willed silently, with all my might. *Please, hold on.*

The auctioneer saw that the boy was weakening and poked at him to make him stand up straight. But it was too late. I gasped as his eyes fluttered open and shut. He uttered a shrill, trilling sound and gave his captors one last questioning look, then fell in a heap, dead on the spot.

In the days and weeks after the boy died, a sadness overtook me, paralyzing my spirit. My life was shadowed by the memory, and I couldn't shake the awful feeling that lay in the pit of my stomach. One day, I finally went to Papa with my pain and a question that had been gnawing at me.

"Didn't you say that in God's sight all human beings was brothers and sisters?" I asked.

"It is so," he answered.

"Then why is it God lets one person buy and own another person? Why do God 'llow slavery?"

Papa pulled me on his lap and hugged me close. "God could, in a blink, make us do everything right, all the time, but that's not how the Almighty works. Let me tell you an old, old story 'bout how God let the first people make their own choices." And with these words, he gently eased my hurt and led me back toward the sunshine.

———◦◦◦———

After the world was put in order, the Lord created a glorious garden named Eden—a heaven right here on the earth. Good weather 'llowed plants and trees of every kind to bloom and bear fruit year round, so food was a-plenty in this perfect place.

Like a loving, caring mother, God brought Adam into being, then placed him in Eden. All the animals came to Adam, and he named each one of them. "You be a horse; you be a monkey; you be a squirrel," and so on. Back then a lamb could cozy up to a lion, and an alligator could side up next to a rooster.

God saw that each of the animals had a mate, but there was no mate for the man. Adam was lonely livin' all by hisself. So, God put the man to sleep and took a rib from his body and made woman. Her name was Eve, and she was Adam's wife.

Adam and Eve were happy in each other's company, a loving couple, for in their garden there was no pain, no suffering, no hatred, no death. Nothing—no, nothing—bad could happen there, 'cause the garden was the Lord's special place for them two special people. Say it was a paradise.

"Live here in Eden in peace and harmony. Swim in the rivers. Eat a-plenty of everything you see," God say, asking only one thing in return. "Don't eat from the tree of the knowledge of good and evil. Y'all can eat everything else, 'cept the fruit from that tree. Don't even touch it, for if you do, you will die."

Listen careful-like to what God said: *Don't even touch it . . . for you will die.*

Meanwhile, Lucifer was paying close attention to God's work, tryin' to figure-on how he could spoil it. I b'lieve Lucifer must be one of God's greatest disappointments. Why? 'Cause God created him.

Imagine Lucifer when he was one of God's brightest angels, full of glory, dazzling to behold. But Lucifer got full of hisself and challenged the Lord's authority in Heaven, so God cast him out where he fell headlong down, down, down into the pit of a burnin' hell. He's known by many names—the Evil One, Ol' Nick, the Devil, Lord of Darkness, and of course, Satan. But the name that fits him best is the Prince of Liars, for Lucifer wouldn't tell the truth if it meant his own salvation.

When Lucifer heard God tell Adam and Eve not to eat from the forbidden tree, right away he commenced to schemin'. Since he couldn't defeat God in Heaven, Lucifer decided he'd ruin things here on the earth.

First he borrowed the body of a snake, which was a beautiful creature that walked upright on its tail back then. Done up like the snake, Lucifer caught

First Lucifer borrowed the body of a snake

Eve when she was alone, probably pickin' berries or flowers that grew everywhere in the garden. He slid up to her, smooth as whale oil, saying, "Haven't
you ever wanted to taste the forbidden fruit?"

"No," replied Eve real simple-like.

But Lucifer was quick with words. "God don't want you to eat from the
tree of the knowledge of good and evil 'cause," he added slyly, "then you'll
know as much as the Lord knows."

That started Eve to thinkin', but she was 'fraid of her own thoughts. "We
were told not to even touch the fruit or we would die."

"No, no, no," Lucifer say, chuckling real wicked-like, his sharp fangs
gleaming. "You won't die." See how fast he lied? "Come, taste the fruit," he
went on. "It won't hurt you none."

Choice. It was all about choice, a plain enough thing to understand. Eve
was at a crossroads. She could yield to temptation and eat the forbidden
fruit, or 'buke Satan and obey God's command. Eve chose, of her own free
will, to eat the fruit. Then she took it to Adam, who had the same choice.
And he ate some of it, too.

At that moment all creation fell to sorrowful weepin' and a-wailin', for
Eden was lost, gone forever!

Adam's and Eve's eyes were opened, and they had the knowledge of
good and evil. For the first time, they realized that they were naked, and they
covered themselves with leaves. They were ashamed. When they heard the
presence of God moving in the garden long about evening time, they tried
to hide.

"Where are you, Adam?" God called.

"Here am I," said Adam, head bowed low. "I was 'shame to come out,
'cause I was naked."

"Who told you that you were naked? Have you eaten the forbidden
fruit?"

Straightaway the man blamed the woman, and the woman put it all on the snake. God knew what really had happened and punished them all.

For 'llowing Lucifer to use its body to do his wicked deed, the snake was forced to crawl on its belly, head in the dust. And for all time there would be a natural-born dislike 'tween snakes and people. Even now today, snakes bite at the heels of Eve's descendants, and human beings are always crushing the head of snakes. But God was also sending a message to Lucifer and makin' Eve a promise. One day one of her descendants would crush the head of sin, and God and humankind would be reconciled again.

But for now, God sentenced the woman to bear children in pain and the man to provide for hisself and his family through the sweat of his brow. Then God drove them from the garden. An angel with a fiery sword stood at Eden's gate to make sure they did not return and eat from the tree of life and live forever. "From dust you came," God told Adam and Eve. "And from dust you shall return after death." Oh, what a sad hour.

Look at what their poor choices had cost them. Life was not near 'bout as good as it had been in the garden. Adam and Eve had to find a place to live, safe from wild animals and bad weather. They had to labor in the fields and grow their food. And Eve suffered the pain of childbirth.

The couple had two sons and they took some joy and comfort in loving and raising them. But even their children continued to make bad choices. Listen to this what I tell you.

Their first son was Cain, who like his father, Adam, tilled the soil. The next was Abel, who was a keeper of sheep.

When it came harvest time, Cain picked up any ol' grains off the ground and laid it 'fore God as an offering. The Lord saw inside Cain's heart and knew that it was not a heartfelt offering, so the Almighty didn't accept it.

Abel went 'fore God with the best of his flock as an offering. God saw what was in Abel's heart and honored him.

Cain's disposition changed after that. He got standoffish. Nothing made him happy. No. God asked him 'bout it, saying, "Why you so angry? If your offering had been worthy, I would've honored it same as I did Abel's."

My, my, my. Cain was so filled with hatred, so filled with jealousy, so filled with meanness, that he decided—he chose—to kill his brother. Yes, he did . . . slipped up and killed his own brother, then buried him, hoping nobody would find out about the sin.

But God has all-seeing eyes. "Where is Abel?" the Lord asked, all the time knowin', but wanting Cain to own up to his crime.

"Am I my brother's keeper?" Cain replied.

"The voice of your brother's blood cries out to me from the ground," say God. "What have you done to him?"

The guilt was all over Cain. He could not deny what had happened, so he admitted it. And God's punishment was fittin' the crime. "Cain, you can farm, but the land will not yield for you no more. You will be cast out, unable to find peace on the earth no matter where you go."

Poor Cain went to beggin' for mercy. "Whoever finds out who I am will kill me. It is more than I can stand, Lord."

"No one will hurt you." Then the Lord set a mark upon Cain's forehead to make sure. "Let it be known throughout the land that whoever kills Cain will feel my vengeance sevenfold."

And Cain left Adam and Eve and went out from the presence of the Lord. He lived in the land of Nod, which was east of Eden.

Listen close when I say Adam and Eve were without sin until they *chose* to disobey God's command. Their children had the same free will. In all the generations numbering from Cain and Abel, brothers have killed brothers and tried to hide it from God or find excuses for doing so. But God is still on the throne—watchin' and takin' tally, and the day of reckoning is a-comin' to all those who bear the mark of Cain. Yes indeed. Yes indeed.

The Big Water

NOAH AND THE FLOOD

Genesis 6, 7, 8; 9:1-12

*E*very summer, Papa went to Belle Isle Plantation, located on a small island off the lowlands, about an hour's row south of Charleston. There, for the whole of a week, he did all the smithing for Daniel O'Brien, a large rice planter. From the time I could walk, I always went along so I could play with Cree, a slave girl my own age who was a friend.

I was twelve the last time I saw Cree. Yet, I have never forgotten her. I can still see her bright eyes and the way her nose crinkled when she laughed. During those short visits we spent hours together, playing Step on Your Shadow, singing, clapping rhythms, running everywhere. Oh, how we loved to run wild and free in the Carolina sea breezes!

All of that changed the summer of 1812. As usual Papa and I went to the island, but when I hurried to the quarters to find Cree, they told me she had been sold away. I asked everybody where she'd gone, but nobody could tell me, not even her poor mama. "Mas' just took her right now," she cried bitterly. "She gone. See her no more."

It was like a death, losing Cree in that way. I tried doing the things we'd always done together, but without her the songs had no joy in them and the running seemed aimless.

"Take heart," Papa said. "I'll put the word out; try to find out who bought Cree. We might not find her, but it'll be worth the try."

Papa wanted to help me feel better. But by the time he had finished his work, my sadness had turned to anger. When we left for the mainland, I promised myself I would never visit Belle Isle Plantation again. With Papa easing into a slow, steady row, the oars dipping and pulling against the dark water, I sat silently, letting my anger grow. Then I made one single wish against all slaveholders. *Oh, God, just swallow 'em up!*

Suddenly, dark clouds appeared on the horizon. Zigzags of lightning flashed in the distance, followed by low, grumbling thunder. The water grew choppy as the wind picked up. Papa rowed faster, toward a tidewater cove. After tying up the boat, we found shelter under a rock ledge. By now the storm was overhead.

"Don't be scared. Spring storms come and go quickly," Papa said. He had spent many years at sea, and understood the ways of the Big Water. But for me, this was no ordinary storm.

"Papa," I said, feeling frightened and guilty, "the Big Water is comin' to get all the slaveholders!"

He smiled. "Is that so? How do you know, Dumplin'?"

"I was angry 'bout Cree, so I asked God to punish all slaveholders, just wipe 'em off the face of the earth."

Papa hugged me up close. "God won't abide with slavery, and one day it will come to an end. But it won't be with the Big Water again."

"How can you be so sure?" I asked.

"Long ago, in the way back times, God made Noah a promise." Then, while we sat huddled underneath the rock ledge waiting for the storm to pass, Papa told me this story.

After Adam and Eve sinned, their children and their children's children went right on sinning—inventing every kind of wrongdoing, including slavery. Their hearts were corrupt, and their minds studied on wickedness from sunup till sundown, day upon day. These were the first generations of mankind, a stubborn people who did not—no, would not—love the Lord.

Meanwhile, God was watching through sad, sad eyes. "I'm sorry I ever made any of them," said the selfsame God who had brought order to the world and set the wheel of eternity a-turning 'round and 'round, no end.

Instead of getting better, the next generation of people got worse! The Lord God's heart was even more filled with regret. But once again, God gave the people every opportunity to do better and turn from their wicked ways. But they were just too wicked, so they rejected God and kept right on sinning.

"There is no hope for them," God said, feelin' a little bit sad. "I'm gon' destroy them all."

It was 'bout then that the Lord noticed Noah and his wife. They were good folk, honest and true, and so were their sons—Shem, Ham, and Japheth. "I am still gon' destroy the earth and all that lives within it, but you and your family will be saved," God told Noah. "Here is my plan. First, you must build an ark, a huge boat that can carry your family and all the animals I plan to save."

I wasn't back there in Noah's time, but I 'spect God's words must have scared Noah mightily. I can almost hear him asking, "Lord, are you gon' destroy *everything*?"

"Everything!" answered the Creator.

That answer left no more doubt in Noah's mind. And straightaway he commenced to buildin' the ark. *Tap, tap, tap.* He used gopher wood, according to God's instructions. *Tap, tap, tap.* How strange Noah must have looked to his neighbors—building a boat far, far 'way from any water. *Tap, tap, tap.* But

Noah didn't care what others thought 'bout him, or what they said. *Tap, tap, tap.* He knew what was coming, and he was getting ready. *Tap, tap, tap.*

In time, Noah finished the ark—built from God's own design. Nobody in those parts had seen anything like it: a seagoing vessel that stood three hundred cubits long and fifty cubits wide. It rose up thirty cubits high, with a window and a door on one side.

God told Noah to gather all kinds of food for him and his family to eat and put that in the boat. Then God said, "Seven pairs of every clean beast, one pair of every unclean beast, and seven pairs of all fowls that live upon the earth will come to you, two by two. Put them all in the ark so they will be saved from the water. Gather food for them to eat also." Noah obeyed.

Soon, two by two—a male and a female of all living creatures, both big and small—showed up at Noah's house. It must have been quite a sight, seeing all them animals marchin' into the ark—deer followin' bears, a pair of mice behind a set of wolves, panthers strutting 'long behind high-steppin' horses, and on and on. Birds of every feather flew in, from the tiny sparrows to the mighty eagles. Noah had to be particular 'bout where he put all them different animals, careful not to place the chickens too close to the foxes, or the rabbits too close to the hawks. Wasn't a soul happy when the crocodiles showed up, not to mention the snakes and the spiders. But there was room on the ark for them as well.

Can't you just hear Noah's neighbors? "Noah is addled for sure." Nobody noticed the storm clouds gathering. They were too busy with riotous livin' and debauchery, don't you know?

At the appointed time, Noah and his wife, their three sons, and their wives went onboard the ark. The Lord Almighty shut the door and locked it just as the first raindrop fell.

The rain started, just a drop or two at first. Then it began to fall in earnest. Right away people could see this was not no regular rain shower like

the ones you get on a summer afternoon. No. No. The sinners cried out for help, but their hearts were not sorry. The wind and rain whispered back: *Too late, sinners! Too, too late. God's judgment is upon you.*

For forty days and forty nights, falls of water poured out of the heavens, and fountains of water gushed up from under the earth. Rivers and streams overflowed; the valleys filled up, and soon even the mountains were covered over. Nothing was left living, 'cept the eight people and animals in the ark, and the fish and great whales that swam alongside it. Noah had built the boat well, for it held 'gainst the raging sea winds, bobbing up and down like a huge barrel. See, God was the pilot who guided it through.

Inside, Noah and his family were warm and dry, but they had their work cut out for them, taking care of all them animals and such. I can't say for sure, but it must have been powerful noisy inside that boat, what with the cows mooing and the cats meowing, the rooster crowing, and the turkeys gobbling—all calling for something to eat, right now!

But at last the rains stopped, and the angry water quieted. The bright sun came out and God sent a gentle wind to dry up the Big Water. First thing, Noah opened up the window and drew in a breath of fresh air. How wonderful that must have felt.

One morning, Noah sent out a raven and a dove to test how far the waters had fallen back. By evening both birds had returned 'cause they were unable to find a dry place to perch.

Day by day, slowly, ever so slowly, the waters ran off. Each morning, Noah sent out the raven and the dove. Each sunset they returned. At last there came an evening when the raven did not come back to the ark. Noah looked out and saw the dark waters still surrounding him. "The raven's wings are strong, and it can fly further than the dove," he said. "It probably found a perch some distance away."

Noah waited seven more days before sending the dove out again. Come

At last the sun came out

evening-time, she flew back with an olive leaf in her beak. Once more and again, Noah waited seven days before sending the dove out. This time she didn't return to the ark.

It wasn't long now. Finally the ark came to rest on the mountains of Ararat. Noah flung open the door of the big boat.

God called the animals forth, saying, "Go out into the world. Be fruitful and multiply, replenish the earth." The eagles flew to the cliffs, and the deer ran to the forests. Bears found caves, and gators took to the swamps. All creatures hurried to their special spot on the earth, where their young ones were born and they live still to this day.

Then God called to Noah and his family. It was time to make a new start. God told them, too, "Be fruitful and multiply." From them the earth would be re-peopled.

When Noah put his feet on solid ground, he commenced to thankin' the Lord for showing him and his family mercy. As he spoke an arc of colors appeared in the sky—red, orange, yellow, blue, green, pink, and purple. And God made a very special promise to Noah and all his descendants. "This rainbow is a sign of my promise to you and all the families that are to come. The world will not be destroyed by water ever again."

Look to the heavens and rejoice! The storm has passed, and the rainbow has appeared to remind us today of that long-ago promise. And listen close. All the hoping and angry wishes in the world can't make God break a promise. On that you can depend.

A Love Worth Waiting For

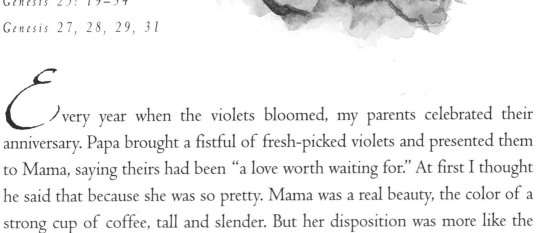

JACOB AND RACHEL

Genesis 17: 1–19

Genesis 21: 1–8

Genesis 25: 19–34

Genesis 27, 28, 29, 31

*E*very year when the violets bloomed, my parents celebrated their anniversary. Papa brought a fistful of fresh-picked violets and presented them to Mama, saying theirs had been "a love worth waiting for." At first I thought he said that because she was so pretty. Mama was a real beauty, the color of a strong cup of coffee, tall and slender. But her disposition was more like the honey she used to sweeten her tea.

Then one spring day, when Papa brought the spring bouquet, I learned the real reason why he felt theirs was a love worth waiting for. It came about when I made a simple request. "How did you come to jump the broom?" I asked Mama after supper.

Mama reached out and touched the little vase of violets in the center of the table. "Well, it all started back in the days when I was still a slave. My mas', Mr. Ames Tillman, sent me to get a kettle repaired at yo' daddy's shop," she said. "When I asked yo' papa how much it would cost, he say, 'Mis Olive, if you just let me see you smile, I'll consider myself well paid.' And I say back to him, 'You fixin' to starve to death charging them kind of prices.'"

Mama's eyes sparkled playfully, and Papa looked a bit embarrassed. Hearing so much joy in my mother's voice made me want to hear more. "When you see Papa again?" I asked.

"He asked to visit me that comin' Sunday," Mama went on, adding that she had to get permission from her mistress. "Mis Tillman 'llowed Price and me to keep company for one hour after church, but I had to make sure all my work was finished."

Mama made hats, which Mis Tillman sold to all the fashionable ladies of Charleston. Of course, Mama never earned a penny from her own labor.

"Yo' Papa was by the bell every Sunday from then on," she said, "bringin' a bouquet of whatever flower was in bloom." Mama paused, and suddenly her mood shifted, her eyes turning downward. "I knew Price Jefferies was gon' ask me to marry him, and sure enough, he did."

"And you say yes!" I blurted out with excitement, ignoring the sadness that had crept across her face. But Mama shook her head. I turned to Papa, whose face had darkened also.

"The slave laws say that if a woman be free, her children be born free. But if a woman's a slave—like I was then—her children's born slaves, too. It make no difference if the father be free or not. I didn't want no child of mine born into slavery. So I turned down the proposal."

Although the idea of Mama and Papa not being together was impossible for me to imagine, I understood her reason, and in a strange way I was pleased. My mother was thinking about me before there even was a me. A loving warmth embraced me, despite the coolness in the early evening air. Papa poked up the fire, and Mama asked me to thread a needle. "Please don't stop now," I begged.

Mama made a few stitches, then pulled the thread through the cloth. "Well, your father offered to buy my freedom for sixty dollars," she said. "But Mr. Tillman wouldn't take less than one hundred dollars."

"Where did Papa get so much money?" I asked.

Mama's eyes followed Papa as he walked to the window and stood with his back to us. "He had some money left over from winning the seamen's lottery and buying his own freedom, but it wasn't enough. He had to work for five long years, night and day," she said, "saving every pence he could. Finally, he earned enough to buy my freedom."

"Then you got married?" I asked. But to my astonishment, the answer was "no" again. "When Papa brought the money to Mr. Tillman, he claimed the price for me was one hundred and ten dollars!"

The news must have been shattering, but I soon learned that the Tillmans' trickery was no match against my mother's own determination to be free.

"For a month I worked all day, sewin' hats for Mis Tillman," she said, her spirits picking up again. "At night I secretly made extra hats—a yellow one with large flowers; blue ones with feathers; green ones with ribbons—a dozen of them, all sizes, all colors. Your father hid them at his shop. Then he took my hats down to the wharf where Captain Robert McEwen, one of his seaman friends, paid five dollars for them. When he learnt the reason, he give me five dollars 'gainst my next batch of hats."

Mama told me that she and Papa jumped the broom a few days later in front of a real preacher. "So you see," she said, touching the violets again and wiping away a happy tear, "these first blooms bring to mind that no matter how cold the winter is, spring always comes. No matter how hard times is, good times will come, too—just like they did for Rachel and Jacob."

"Who's Rachel and Jacob?" I asked curiously.

Papa returned to the table. He had been quiet while Mama talked, only nodding or smiling from time to time. He poked up the fire again. "I reckon Jacob felt 'bout Rachel like I do 'bout yo' mama," he said. "Theirs was a love worth waiting for, too."

I snuggled up close because I knew it was time for him to tell one of the old, old stories.

One of the most beautiful love stories of all times is 'bout Jacob and Rachel. It begins with Jacob's grandfather, Abram, long back in Bible times, after the beginning and after the Flood.

God spoke to Abram, who lived in a far-off country, saying, "Leave the land of your mother and father and go to a new place I'll show you."

Always the faithful servant, Abram obeyed God and became a traveling man, living in a tent under an open sky. Say his kinfolks didn't understand this and asked, "Abram, where you goin' and how you gon' get there?"

"God will provide," is all Abram would say.

After many wanderings and adventures, Abram came to live in the land of Canaan. God spoke to him again. Say, "From now on you will go by the name of Abraham, what means 'father of many,' and your wife, Sarai, will be called Sarah, what means 'princess.' And I will make you a promise. The land you see 'fore you will be your descendants' land for all time. You two will be the father and mother of many nations."

Abraham say, "Lord, I am a very old man, near 'bout ninety. Sarah is as old. How we gon' have children?"

God showed Abraham the stars. "Hear me. Yo' descendants will be as many as the lights that are in the heavens."

Abraham was respectful of the Lord in all ways. But he couldn't help but wonder how all this was gon' happen. When he told Sarah, she laughed. "I'm far too old to bear children," she said, not believing it was possible. Sarah was only laughing to hide the hurt. More than anything she wanted a child.

And sure enough, in time, Sarah and Abraham were blessed with a son. They named the boy Isaac—what means "laughter." He brought his parents great happiness, and filled their lives with love and joy.

Listen close now to the story of Isaac, who grew up and married Rebekah. God told Isaac the same thing he told Abraham. "Yo' descendants shall be as many as the stars in the heavenly sky."

When Rebekah was with child, she felt two babies strugglin' inside her. She asked God what the meaning of this was.

God answered: "You carrying two nations. They will be born as two babies, but they'll go different ways through life. The older twin will be stronger, but the younger one will be placed over his brother."

Not long afterward, Rebekah gave birth to twins. Esau come first, followed by Jacob, who was born holding his brother's heel.

Rebekah never let on 'bout what God had said. She kept it all in her heart and studied on it. Meanwhile, Jacob grew up kind and gentle—a quiet, good-natured boy. Rebekah knew God had a plan for him, so she took Jacob to heart. On the other hand, Isaac favored Esau; he was a strong, fun-loving boy who became a good hunter. He kept his father's cooking pot bubbling, and that pleased Isaac just fine.

One day, Esau came home from a hunt with a fierce appetite in his belly. Jacob had fixed a big pot of stew, and it was smelling good. "Give me something to eat for I am starving," pleaded Esau.

"Sell me your birthright—the rights that belong to the firstborn son—and I will feed you," Jacob answered.

Esau let his hunger make the decision rather than using his head. He blurted out, "Done! What good is my birthright when I am starving now?" He would live to be sorry for saying that. Mercy me.

Years slipped by, one, then another and another. Father Isaac grew old and near 'bout blind. Death was close at hand so, according to custom, he made ready to bless his oldest son. "Fix my favorite venison stew," he told Esau. "I will eat it and bless you in the presence of the Lord."

Rebekah overheard the plan and conjured up a scheme to help Jacob get the blessing meant for Esau. While Esau was away hunting, she had Jacob stir up a meal for old Isaac. "Take this to your father," she said.

"But he will know it is not me," said Jacob.

"Sell me your birthright and I will feed you," Jacob answered.

Rebekah had already thought of that. She gave Jacob several pieces of goatskin. "Yo' brother's hairy. When Isaac asks you to come close, put these over your arms and around yo' neck. He will touch them and think you be Esau."

Jacob went to his father with the dish of stew and fresh-made bread.

"Who is it?" old Isaac asked.

"It is Esau, yo' eldest son," Jacob said, deceiving his father.

Remember now, Isaac was old and blind. Still, he knew something wasn't quite right. "You don't sound like Esau. Come closer, let me touch you. Let me smell you."

Jacob had done what his mother'd said. He had put on Esau's clothing and covered his arms with the animal skin. Isaac smelled his shoulders and felt his hands and he was fooled.

Isaac ate the stew, then he blessed Jacob—which meant Jacob stood to inherit everything that was Isaac's with his father's blessing.

When Esau learned about the trickery, he promised to kill Jacob as soon as Isaac died. Rebekah acted quickly, helping Jacob escape before any harm could come to him. "Go to my brother's house," she said. "Once Esau has gotten over his anger, I will send for you."

Jacob quickly left the land of his grandfather Abraham and his father, Isaac, taking only what he had on his back. After Jacob had traveled some distance, he came to a place where he decided to spend the night, using a rock as a pillow. Say, yes he did. A rock.

What a glorious dream he had that night! He saw a ladder stretching from Heaven down to the earth. Angels climbed up and down this ladder. Can't you see angels a-movin' around up there? Can't you hear them singin' with a sweetness? What a sight and sound that must have been.

In the dream, the Lord Almighty spoke to Jacob. Say, "I am the God of your grandfather Abraham and your father, Isaac. I make the same promise to you that I made to them. Yo' descendants will be countless and spread all over the earth, for they are a people truly blessed."

Come first light, Jacob knew that he had slept in a holy place. He called it Bethel, what mean "House of God."

Jacob quit Bethel and headed for Haran, where his uncle Laban lived.

Rachel, the daughter of Laban, was a shepherdess. She had brought her father's flock to the well to be watered just 'bout the time Jacob come up. When Jacob's eye fell on sweet Rachel, he was smitten with the joy of love. The Bible don't say just so, but I s'pose Rachel loved Jacob right back.

As his mother had say do, Jacob told his uncle everything that had happened back in Canaan. "You are my sister's son," said Laban. "You are welcome to stay with me."

After a month or so had passed, Laban say to Jacob, "You shouldn't work for me without pay. Name your wages."

This was Jacob's chance. He loved Rachel with all his heart and more than anything he wanted her to be his wife. He say to Laban, "I will become your servant for seven years to earn the right to marry your youngest daughter, Rachel." Laban agreed easy enough.

True to his word, Jacob gave Laban the full measure of his labor, increasing Laban's herds and multiplying his wealth three-fold. Jacob did all that was required of him with a cheerful heart, 'cause having Rachel as his beloved bride was gon' be his reward.

To mark the time, I imagine Jacob and Rachel made all kinds of plans, talking and sharing, wondering 'bout what it was gon' be like when they was together for always. Season into season, Jacob must have had a way of watching the time until the years numbered seven. And with the long wait behind him at last, Jacob asked for Rachel's hand.

But Laban turned to trickery. He fooled po' Jacob into marrying Leah, his oldest daughter, by hiding her behind the wedding veil. When Jacob raised it and discovered he wasn't married to Rachel, his heart was broke in two. Wasn't that there was anything wrong with Leah, but she wasn't Rachel. For Jacob, nobody else would do. He went to Laban asking for a reason.

"Listen to me, " Laban said in a soothing voice. "Please understand, it is our custom that the oldest daughter should be married first. I couldn't let Rachel marry before her sister Leah. Remember, you can have more than one wife. You may still marry Rachel, *in seven days,* but you've got to promise to work for me *seven more years.*" You see, Jacob was a fine laborer, and Laban didn't want to let him go.

So Jacob agreed to Laban's terms, even though his father-in-law had cheated him. In time, Jacob got over his anger. His herds increased and so did his family. He had other wives, but Rachel was always his favorite. Theirs was a true love, the kind that is always worth waiting for.

How Can You Forgive?

THE STORY OF JOSEPH

Genesis 37, 39, 40, 41, 42, 43, 44, 45, and 46

Boys sometimes came to the forge in hopes of earning a penny or two doing chores or enjoying one of Papa's stories. "Come let me tell you 'bout a man whose donkey talked to him," Papa'd begin, inviting them to hear Balaam's Donkey. Or, "Did you ever hear the story 'bout Joshua who fit the battle of Jehrico?"

Jesse was my favorite of all the boys. He was new to Charleston and seemed to need liking more than the others. Although he was no more than nine or ten, he had old eyes. There was so much sorrow and pain in them, I felt like crying for him without really knowing why. Then I heard him say he had been sold away from his mother and father, and I began to understand.

One day Jesse brought one of his master's tools to the forge to be repaired. He came at lunchtime, so I asked him to stay and share a fish and biscuit with me. As we ate our lunch, I asked Jesse why he had been sold, hoping my question was not too personal.

He didn't seem to mind talking about it. "Two slaves, Bob Edward and Lizzie, from back at my old plantation in Virginny, wanted to get married," he said, "but Mas' wouldn't have it. They knowed I could write, so they begged me to make them out a runaway pass.

"I wrote a note and signed my massa's name to it. That gave Lizzie and Bob Edward permission to be on the road. They used the fake note to get away. It would'a worked, too, if'n Mas' hadn't come back early from his trip. He set the dogs after the runaways and caught 'em. But he was mo' worried 'bout who had learnin' enough to write that note than anything 'bout running 'way. To keep from gettin' beat, they told on me. I got the worstest whuppin' you can think of, and then I got sold 'way—far 'way—from my folks."

I was furious. "Don't you hate Bob Edward and Lizzie for telling on you?" I shouted angrily.

"At first I did," he answered simply. "But I studied on it. I figured they wasn't all to blame. Put in their place I might would'a done the same thing. In time I forgave Lizzie and Bob Edward—first in my head, then in my heart."

After Jesse had gone I told Papa what he had said. "How do you find forgiveness for something so awful?" I asked.

"Joseph must have asked that same question of hisself a hundred times," Papa said.

"Tell me 'bout Joseph," I said, hoping the story would help me understand. I climbed up on a low-hanging branch of our live oak and listened. And as Papa mended a skillet, he told me a story about mending the heart with forgiveness.

Joseph's story begins long ago,

after the beginning,

after Adam and Eve,

after Noah and the Flood,

after Abraham and Sarah,

after Isaac and Rebekah,

and after Jacob had worked for Laban for many a year. At last, Jacob went back to Canaan with his four wives, eleven sons, and one daughter. Esau forgave him for stealing his blessing and welcomed his brother home again. Isaac, their father, was dead, and so was their mother, Rebekah. But Jacob still didn't quite trust Esau, so he chose to live near Bethel, where he had seen the ladder to Heaven.

Sadly, Rachel died shortly after giving birth to her second son, Benjamin, and Jacob could not—no, he would not—be comforted. Once again the Lord spoke to Jacob and told him to be strong. Say, "You are going to be the father of a great nation. And your name from now on will be Israel."

Now, Israel was the proud father of twelve sons—Reuben, Simeon, Levi, Judah, Zebulun, and Issachar, Dan, Gad, Asher, and Naphtali, Joseph, and Benjamin.

Poor Israel mourned the loss of his beloved Rachel, and he poured all the love he had for her on Joseph, Rachel's firstborn. The boys grew jealous of this favorite son, even though Joseph loved them. Israel made matters worse when he gave Joseph a fine cloak of dazzling colors—red, orange, green, yellow, and blue. Joseph put the cloak on and paraded 'round in front of the others. Father Israel was pleased that his son loved the gift, never once noticin' that his older sons were angry.

"I am the oldest!" said Reuben. "And Father's not given me a fine gift."

"Nor I," added Levi.

Then Joseph commenced to having dreams that fanned the fires of their anger. "We was working in the fields," he told his brothers, "when your bundles of wheat bowed down to mine. What do you think it means?"

Reuben threw his arms up real disgusted-like. "So you b'lieve you will one day lord over us, and have us bow down to you!"

"No," said Joseph. "I don't want to rule over you." But in time, Joseph had another dream. "The sun, moon, and eleven stars bowed down to me," he said.

That one near 'bout took Israel's breath a-way. "Are you to be over yo' mother, your father, and all your brothers, too?" he asked. Joseph's dreams were troubling to Israel, 'cause he remembered how God had often spoke to him in dreams.

I'm first to admit that Joseph may have been difficult for others to understand, but he was only seventeen and had not yet learnt to use his gift wisely. The more Joseph told of his dreams, the more his brothers fumed and fussed and carried on. They boiled in their pot of spite until it was ready to bubble over.

"Here comes the dreamer now," said Asher one day as they tended the cattle and sheep out in the field and away from their father's tent.

"Let's kill him," said Simeon.

"We could do it and say a wild animal killed him," said Dan.

They plotted and planned against Joseph, and *would* have killed him, weren't for Reuben steppin' in.

"Let's throw the boy in the well," he suggested, all the time plannin' to come back and free his little brother.

So they snatched off Joseph's colorful robe and threw him into a deep, dark well. Meanwhile, Reuben went to tend sheep some distance away, leavin' the others to watch Joseph 'til he got back.

"Please, brothers, help me. Have mercy on me!" the boy cried pitifully. But his brothers' hearts were without mercy.

Long 'bout that time, a caravan passed on the way to Egypt. *Tingle, tingle, tingle,* the bells on the camel bags sounded softly in the winds.

"I got an idea," said Judah. "Let's sell him to the traders." And they sold their own brother into slavery before Reuben returned.

The traders pulled Joseph from the well. "He will make a fine slave."

"There must be a mistake," said Joseph. "Please have mercy. Take me to my father and he will pay you good money for returnin' me."

But the traders laughed, and the sons of Israel turned their backs on their brother as he was taken away.

"Now we rid of him," they said to one another.

When Reuben came back, he was horrified to see what had happened.

To cover up their deed, the brothers killed a lamb and soaked Joseph's cloak in its blood. Then they returned home and told their father that Rachel's son had been killed by a wild beast.

The hurt cut deep into the old man's heart, and he grieved mightily for his lost boy. "My son," Jacob cried. "My po', po' son. See him no more." Oh, the tears that have been shed for lost children could form a new sea.

By this time, the traders had reached Egyptland, and Joseph had done been bought by a captain of Pharaoh's guard. Potiphar was his name. He took an interest in the boy and, after a while, placed Joseph over his house and business. Things went along nicely 'til Potiphar's wife told a vicious lie on Joseph—say he made ungentlemanly advances toward her. Potiphar took his wife's word and sent Joseph to prison.

Even there, Joseph never lost hope, never lost faith. In time, the jailers saw his goodness and placed him over the other prisoners, saying, "Whatever Joseph say do, do it. Whatever Joseph say don't do, don't do it."

The royal butler and the royal baker were also in prison, 'longside Joseph. One morning, Joseph noticed that the two men looked more upset than usual.

"What ails you?" Joseph asked.

"Please have mercy," cried Joseph.

"I had a strange dream last night," said the butler.

"Tell it to me."

The butler say, "In my dream, I saw a vine with three branches. I was picking and squeezing the grapes in a cup and putting it in Pharaoh's hand."

Joseph explained, "The branches of the vine represent three days. In three days you will be called back to the side of Pharaoh and you will pour his wine again."

"Thank you, thank you," said the butler.

"Just remember me when you are free."

Hearing all this, the baker commenced to tell Joseph his dream. He seen three white baskets on his head. Birds had been eating from the top basket.

Joseph looked at the baker sadly. "Your fate is death. In three days you will be hung, and the birds shall eat your flesh."

Three days later, on Pharaoh's birthday, the royal butler was forgiven and the royal baker was hung.

Once back in the good graces of Pharaoh, the butler forgot all 'bout Joseph, completely forgot. Joseph stayed in prison for two more years.

It was 'bout then that Pharaoh started having strange dreams. He sought guidance from all the wise men and magicians throughout the kingdom, but none could tell him what his dreams meant. Upon hearing of Pharaoh's problem, the butler remembered Joseph and told Pharaoh about him.

Pharaoh sent for the prisoner. "My butler say you interpret dreams."

"It is none of my doing. God gives me the understanding," Joseph said, taking no credit for his gift.

"Then pray ask your God to tell me the meaning of these."

Joseph listened. "In my first dream," Pharaoh began, "seven fat cows come from the river. Then seven starving cows come from the river. The seven starving cows swallow up the seven fat ones whole. Still, the starving cows stay thin and weak."

Worry lines creased the mighty king's forehead. He studied the room, looking from one counselor to another, hoping one would speak up. But all they could do was drop their heads, for they had no understanding.

Pharaoh closed his eyes and went on, saying, "There is a second dream that always follows the first. I sleep again, and I see seven ears of corn growing on one stalk. Then seven thin ears grow up alongside them, and they are blasted by the hot desert wind. Then the seven thin ears devour the healthy ears of corn. I awake and see it is a dream, a troubling dream." He forced his eyes open. He looked rung out, weak with worry.

The Lord Almighty put the words of wisdom in Joseph's mouth, and he spoke with authority. He say, "The two dreams are really one. There will be seven good years when the land will yield up its bounty. There will be plenty for everyone. But there will follow seven bad years when the land will lay dry and barren, and hunger will visit every household."

Joseph didn't stop there, but spoke right up to the king of Egypt. "If you have a wise and honest man in your service, have him store up food during the years of plenty. Come the seven bad years, there will be enough to make it through the hard times."

The king looked into Joseph's eyes. "I have found that wise and honest man," he said. "It is you."

Pharaoh gave Joseph his ring and put him over all the land, second only to Pharaoh hisself. "Whatever Joseph say do, do it. Whatever Joseph say don't do, don't do it," Pharaoh commanded the people of Egypt. And they obeyed.

Joseph went ahead with his work, gathering a portion of all the grains that were harvested. And sure enough, famine came to the land in seven years. Joseph threw open the storehouses, and there was plenty for all.

Remember now, Joseph was barely a man—seventeen, to be exact—when he was sold into Egypt. He was thirty when Pharaoh made him governor of the land. Joseph hadn't seen or heard from his family in all that time.

He didn't know that down through the years, Father Israel had grieved for him. He didn't know that his eleven brothers now had families and were all living in Canaan. And he didn't know that mean times had come to Canaan as well—their wells had done dried up, and so had their fields. Nothing grew, so there was nothing to eat, nothing to feed the livestock, either.

And Joseph didn't know that his father, having heard there was no hunger in Egypt, had sent his sons there to buy food for the family.

Reuben, Simeon, Levi, Judah, Zebulun, Issachar, Dan, Gad, Asher, and Naphtali set off. Israel would not allow Benjamin to go 'cause he was Rachel's only remaining son. "If something happens to him," said ol' Israel, "then I will die."

Now the sons of Israel come to Egyptland. They stood 'fore the mighty governor of Egypt. Not a one of them recognized him as their own flesh 'n' blood brother. Joseph knew them, though, but he held his tongue.

"Help us," Reuben cried.

"Have mercy on us," said Judah. "We've come to buy food for our families in Canaan."

They fell on their knees and bowed down to Joseph. Many years had passed, but Joseph's dreams had come true! Here were his brothers bowing down to him. They looked so humble now, not at all as he remembered them, angry and hateful.

Joseph wanted to tell them who he was, but he decided to wait. These were the selfsame brothers who had thought of killing him. What had they done to his father? To Benjamin? He had to be sure.

Joseph asked his brothers questions about their father. Who was he? How was he gettin' 'long and all?

The sons of Israel fell on their knees

"Our father is Israel, the son of Isaac, who was the son of Abraham. We left him in Canaan, where he is old but well," said Simeon.

"Do you have any other brothers?" Joseph asked.

Simeon told him about Benjamin and that he was back home.

Joseph decided to test his brothers. "Spies—all of you are spies!" he cried. He pointed at Simeon. "You will stay here while the others go get the one known as Benjamin. You must prove to me that you speak the truth about this brother before I will release you."

"We are not spies! We have nothing to hide," Simeon went to beggin'. "We are the sons of Israel and we come in peace."

The words sounded right, but Joseph still wondered if his brothers had learned to love and protect each other. They had sold him into slavery 'cause they were jealous. Would they come back for Simeon? Or would they leave him to rot in an Egyptian prison?

After selling them food, Joseph secretly returned their money. When the brothers found the money in their bags, they were confused and frightened. Who was this strange governor of Egypt? What did he want with Benjamin?

Nine brothers hurried back to Canaan. It took a powerful lot of convincing, but Israel finally let Benjamin go back with them. When Joseph saw all his brothers kneeling 'fore him again, he was pleased. How sweet it was to see them all, especially Benjamin. Joseph wanted to rush to him and hug him 'round the neck, but still he held back. Instead, Joseph asked them to sup with him.

Oh, and it was a grand feast, laid out a-plenty. But to make sure that his brothers had changed from their hateful ways, Joseph had yet one more test of their character. While they were eatin' and drinkin' he hid a silver cup in Benjamin's sack. Yes, he did that.

The next morning the brothers left. Imagine how surprised they were when their host sent soldiers after them to search their sacks. "You have

stolen from the lord governor," said the soldiers, and of course they soon found the silver cup Joseph had hidden.

The soldiers took Benjamin back, but he was not alone. All the brothers returned with him. When Joseph saw this, he was even more pleased than before, yet he pretended to be angry. "You are a thief," he accused Benjamin.

"But I did not take the silver cup. I would not steal," said Benjamin.

"The one who took my cup will become my slave!"

"No, not Benjamin," they all cried out.

"Make me your slave," pleaded Judah. "Our father lost his favorite son, Joseph, many years past, and still he grieves. I could not bear to see him lose another, for he will surely die."

Joseph looked at Judah long and hard. This was the brother who had suggested that he be sold into slavery. Judah had changed; indeed they all had changed. "Have you ever wondered what happened to your brother Joseph?"

Silence.

"Behold I am that brother."

I imagine they was all took by surprise and shock and fell on their knees before their brother and begged his forgiveness. I reckon I can hear brother Judah speaking up, saying, "No! What we did to you was wrong. We don't deserve to be forgiven."

"Rise up," Joseph said to them kindly. "Let the past lie still in the past. The bad that you did to me, God has turned it into good. Go, bring my father and your families here to Egypt."

Now, if Joseph could forgive his brothers for the wrong they done to him, then maybe we can be more forgiving, too.

When Joseph's family arrived, Pharaoh welcomed them and set aside land for them called Goshen. Israel was reunited with Joseph, and the tears flowed freely. And they all kneeled down before him out of gratitude and respect, just like Joseph the dreamer said it would happen.

God Will Not Hold with Wrong

MOSES AND THE EXODUS

The Book of Exodus
Deuteronomy 5, 9:6–29, 29
Numbers 13, 14, 33

*O*ne afternoon I was playing under the willow fronds just beyond the wood-pile, listening to the familiar ring of my father's hammer as it fell against the anvil. *Clink! Clank! Clink!* Papa was making a horseshoe, so he didn't see or hear the stranger who approached. But I did. He looked like other captains I had seen, so I guessed he was a seaman—perhaps a man Papa had served with.

Clink! Clank! Clink! The man paused as though he was uncertain of his next move. Then he called Papa's name. "Kisse Price."

Papa jerked around; "Kisse" was his African name, to which "Price" had been added when he became Captain Price's slave aboard the *Gabriel.* Only those who knew him back then ever called him that. Papa'd since changed his surname to Jefferies—in honor of the Reverend Silas Jefferies, who'd taught him his trade. Then he let Price become his first name.

I saw recognition in Papa's expression, followed by a strange mixture of sadness and surprise. Who was this man? I wondered. I drew nearer to get a

better look and maybe even hear what they were saying.

"You've done well for yeself, Kisse—or is it Price Jefferies, now?" The seaman chuckled softly over his words. "I see you've taken my surname as your first."

So this must be the notorious Captain Shelby Price, my father's old master in the flesh, I realized. I had heard plenty about Captain Price, and everything I'd heard was bad. I moved in even closer, finding a perfect hiding spot behind the woodpile.

I remembered Papa telling me that Berber traders had stolen him from his African home when he was a young boy and sold him to Captain Price. For over fifteen years Papa had served as Captain Price's personal slave onboard the slaver, the *Gabriel.*

Papa turned the horseshoe over and went back to pounding. *Clink! Clink! Clank!*

"I've come because I wanted you to know I got r'ligion 'bout a month ago and I'm tryin' to make amends for my misdoings. Gave up hard whiskey, gave up swearing, and I've quit slaving completely; got no more stomach fer it. Now I'm standing before you, man to man, saying I'm sorry. I'm sorry for keeping you as a slave. That I am."

Papa spoke to Captain Price calmly and quietly. I couldn't believe how civil he was being to his old master. "You made a good start. What else you planning to do?"

The captain laughed, but I could see he was not amused. "What do you mean? I've given up my own personal slaves and my business of twenty years," he said, shifting his weight from foot to foot. "And I've humbled myself before you. What more am I expected to do?"

"After all you done, saying you sorry aine near 'bout enough," Papa replied. "You must work to rid the land of slavery." Papa pounded the metal harder. *Clink! Clink! Clank!* "If a man like you who's been a slaver speaks out,

others will be bound to listen. Do that, and you might find the peace you seek."

The look on Captain Price's face hardened. His eyes were dark pools of anger. I could only imagine what horrors my father had endured on his ship.

"I'll not have the likes of you telling me what I must do!" he cried. Then, sucking in his breath as if to control himself, and speaking in a condescending tone, he went on. "Slavery is an old, old business, Kisse, found all over this world. Even your own people keep slaves. I've rid my life of it. But slavery will be around forever."

"That's where you're wrong," Papa responded. He pounded the metal harder. *Clink! Clink! Clank!* "Just as God heard the Israelites' cries for freedom from Pharaoh a long way back, so the Almighty hears my people's pleas today. Whose side you want to be on when God's judgment comes?"

Captain Price threw up his hands to stop Papa's words, and said through clenched teeth, "You test my patience, Kisse!" Then he moved in close and pointed his finger at Papa. "I came here to say I was sorry because that's what the good pastor said I should do. I've done it, now. Push me no further!"

Papa slammed the hammer down on the red-hot metal, shaping it. *Clink! Clink! Clank!* "With or without your help, Captain, one day we will *all* be free."

Suddenly, everything became so quiet, I could hear the fish crows fussing in the bell tower of the church a block away. Captain Price parted his lips as if he wanted to say more, but turned instead and hurried away.

Papa began hammering again. *Clink! Clank! Clank!* "You may come from behind the woodpile, Charlotte."

During the entire confrontation between my father and his former master I had hardly moved or even breathed. I was surprised that he knew I was there, and fearful he'd be angry with me for eavesdropping. I slowly sidled over. But Papa just kept right on with his work.

At last I ventured to speak. "Papa, how come you so sure slavery will end?" I asked, anxious to talk about what I'd overheard.

"'Cause God created all people free and equal. Slavery's wrong," he answered. "And God will not hold with wrong, never mind how right folks think they be."

"How long you think slavery gon' last?" I asked.

Papa shook is head. "I'm mighty 'fraid bad times got to come to this land 'fore it'll be over. It's all in the story of Moses."

I had heard about Moses before. "He's the one that led the Hebrew people out of slavery in Egypt," I said, feeling proud that I knew that much.

Papa dunked the white-hot horseshoe in a barrel of water, and steam billowed above the rim. The metal was set. He lifted me to the top of the woodpile, then picked up another piece of metal. And there in the shade of the live oak, I listened to him tell the powerful story of Moses while he fashioned a formless shape into a thing of beauty. *Clink! Clink! Clank . . .*

The Good Book say that in time there came to power a new Pharaoh who didn't know Joseph. The descendants of Israel's sons had become known as Hebrews, and they had multiplied generation after generation. They were now a large nation living inside the larger nation of Egypt. This Pharaoh saw the thousands and thousands of Hebrews living in Goshen. And he grew fearful that they would become too strong and overthrow him. So he made them slaves and tried to break their will under the lash.

Even though Hebrews were forced to work, building Egypt's great monuments and cities, they kept faith with God and believed that one day they would be delivered from their suffering and oppression. They continued to have children, and their children had children.

As their numbers increased, so did Pharaoh's fear of them. Now he reached way back into a dark corner of his mind and found a wicked and cowardly idea. "I want every male Hebrew child killed at birth," he ordered. "Kill them all!"

Oh the cry that went up out of Goshen! The wailing and the moaning that rose to Heaven was a sound so pitiful, it must have saddened the very heart of the living God.

Now, Amram and Jochebed were descendants of Levi, one of ol' Israel's sons. God blessed the couple with a baby boy. To keep him from being slaughtered with the other Hebrew innocents, they kept him a secret. But Jochebed knew that the time was coming when she could no longer hide her baby. God helped her by giving Jochebed a plan.

Night after night Jochebed worked on making a basket of river reeds, the same way women weave the sweet grasses here in Charleston. In and out, in and out, around and around, Jochebed built the basket.

Her daughter, Miriam, watched. "What you gon' put in the basket?" the girl asked.

"You'll see."

Then the mother covered the bottom with tar so the basket could float.

The next morning, Jochebed laid her baby in the watertight basket, set it on the Nile River, and gave it a little push. "God will take care of him," she told Miriam. "Watch to see what happens."

Miriam stayed behind to watch the basket float down the river to where Pharaoh's daughter was bathing. "Oh," said the princess when she saw it, "what a beautiful baby!"

The princess didn't have no children of her own, so she took him to be hers. She say, "I will call him Moses, 'cause it means 'taken from the water.'"

Meanwhile, Miriam ran home and told her family all that she had seen and heard. She was sad that her brother could not grow up with her, but she was contented, knowin' he was safe.

Moses grew to manhood in Pharaoh's household, living in splendor and wealth, oh, you can't imagine. No. He had the best learnin', the best food, the best clothing, the best of everything laid at his feet. But in his heart, Moses always felt that the way the Egyptians treated the Hebrews was wrong.

One day Moses saw an Egyptian beating a Hebrew slave. Moses killed the Egyptian to save the slave's life. Moses didn't think anybody had seen him, but somebody had. And to make matters worse, they took it to Pharaoh.

Since the penalty for murder was death, Moses fled from Egypt, thinking he'd never return again. All of his life Moses had lived in the court of a mighty king. Now he stood alone, facing the wilderness. Oh, the idea of it makes you weep until you understand that Moses was part of a much grander plan that had yet to unfold.

Po' Moses wandered for days upon days, hot under the blindin' sun and shiverin' from cold at night. There was no mercy in the burnin' desert sands, but he pushed on, stumblin' over rocks and thistle bushes, watchin' out for the snakes and scorpions—until at last, he came to Midian. There he sat by a well, thankful to have water.

Seven women, the daughters of Jethro, came to the well to water their sheep. Moses watched as several shepherds come there with their flock. "Get back and out of the way," one said, shoving ahead of the women. "We will water our sheep first."

Moses spoke up for the women. "You should wait your turn."

"Who will stop us?"

"I will!" And Moses jumped right in with his staff, beat off the shepherds, and watered the women's sheep hisself.

The women rushed home to tell their father. "An Egyptian took our part 'gainst the shepherds.'"

"Go get this man," said Jethro, "so that we can thank him properly." Jethro invited Moses into his tent and fed him.

For near 'bout forty years Moses made a life for himself in Midian—even married Zipporah, one of Jethro's seven daughters. They had a son, who was named Gershom. I imagine Moses would have stayed right there for the rest of his days, but God had other work for him to do.

Moses was watching his sheep on Mount Horeb, the mountain of God, when suddenly he heard something crackling like it was on fire. He turned to see a bush burning—but it didn't burn up. What a sight to see, wonderful and frightening all at the same time! Full of fear and trembling, Moses crept forward.

That's when God spoke to him. "Take off your shoes, Moses. You on holy ground."

Moses obeyed with a quickness.

Then God say, "I am the God of Abraham, Isaac, and Jacob. I have heard my people in Egypt cry out to me for help. They are beaten down, mistreated, and suffering. Now, I tell you Moses, go and bring my people out of Egypt so they can worship me in the desert."

It wasn't hard to understand. God was 'bout to free the Hebrews from slavery in Egypt and had chosen Moses to do it! But, now, Moses didn't want to hear that. "Lord," Moses asked, "when Pharaoh asks who sent me, what am I to say?"

"Tell Pharaoh I AM, that I AM sent you."

"But why me, Lord?" Moses was determined to convince God that he wasn't the one to send.

"I will be with you," God promised.

Still, Moses had to put in a word. He told the Lord he didn't speak well and sometimes stuttered.

"Moses, I'm gon' help you speak," God said, getting a bit peevish. "Yo' brother Aaron can help you. And I will always be with you both. Now go!"

Finally, Moses hushed up and made ready to go back to Egyptland.

He found his family still living in Goshen. After telling Aaron 'bout God's plan, they went to see Pharaoh. Moses stood before the great king, saying, "God gave me these words to deliver to you: 'Let my people go so that they may make sacrifices to me in the desert.'"

Pharaoh's heart was hard, and he laughed. "Who is this God of slaves? I will not let the Hebrews go. They are lazy and don't want to work. Now I won't give them straw to make bricks. Let them find their own straw, and the number they are expected to make each day must stay the same."

Naturally, the Hebrew slaves couldn't find straw *and* make their tally, so that gave the overseers cause to beat them harder. "Look at what has happened to us on account of you, Moses!" the people cried.

Moses was discouraged. "Lord, I have made matters worse. What shall I do? Oh, what shall I do?"

"Go back to Pharaoh and tell him to let my people go! Don't be surprised if he won't listen to you, for Pharaoh's heart will be hard. But when he sees my power, he will free my people."

Pharaoh did laugh—loud and long. "I will not let the Hebrews go nowhere," he scoffed, and dismissed them with a wave of his hand.

"Then see the power of God," Moses said, throwing down his staff. At once, it coiled into a hissing snake. Pharaoh laughed again. "A trick! My court magicians can do the same thing." And he ordered one to throw down his staff. When the magician did, it became a snake. But Moses' snake ate up the other snake. Hard-hearted Pharaoh saw God's power, but he still would not obey.

The next day, Pharaoh went to the Nile River to ask the river god to bless the water. Moses and Aaron followed him there. Aaron spoke the words Moses had told him. "Pharaoh, God say, 'Let my people go.'"

Hard-hearted Pharaoh laughed yet again. He shouted, "I know nothing 'bout your God. Leave me!"

Moses gave his staff to Aaron and told him to hold it over the Nile. Suddenly, the water turned to blood. Yes it did. The water in Pharaoh's house also turned to blood. And the water in every Egyptian cup and vase turned to blood. Only the Israelites had fresh water to drink.

"There is no water," the Egyptians cried out. Seven long, thirsty days passed. Moses and Aaron went back to Pharaoh. "Are you ready to listen, now? God say, 'Let my people go.'"

Hard-hearted Pharaoh would not be moved. "I will never let the Hebrew slaves go! Tell that to yo' God."

Moses told Aaron to hold the staff over the water again. This time the blood was gone. But—*croak, croak, croak!* Frogs by the thousands hopped out of the river. *Croak!* They jumped everywhere. There were frogs in the gardens. *Croak!* Frogs in the houses. Frogs in the kitchens. There were frogs even in Pharaoh's bed. *Croak!* But there were no frogs in the Hebrews' houses.

Pharaoh saw God's power once again, but he still wouldn't obey the command: "Let my people go." So God sent lice to plague Egypt. They bit the Egyptians and they bit the Egyptians' animals. Ol' Pharaoh himself was itchin' and scratchin', but he still refused to free the Hebrews. Then God sent the plague of flies upon Egypt—flies, flies, and more flies, but Pharaoh hung on to his stubbornness like a dog with a bone.

The people of Egypt were visited by all manner of plagues on account of Pharaoh's hard heart. Their animals got sick; folk got sores all over their bodies; then came burnin' hail, followed by a swarm of locusts. Yet after all these signs, Pharaoh *still* would not obey God's command. But when God blocked the sun for three days, Pharaoh got scared. He and his people had suffered mightily. "All we want is for the Hebrews to go 'way and leave us be," he told Moses.

But then Pharaoh's heart was hardened again, and he changed his mind. "No! If I free the slaves, who will do our work, build our cities and monuments?"

Frogs jumped everywhere

Now God said to Moses, "Tell the Hebrews to do this. Between dusk and darkness, each family should kill a flawless lamb or a kid. Put some of the blood on their doorposts and lintels. Tonight the firstborn of every Egyptian will die. But the Destroyer will not enter the house of those whose homes are protected by the blood of the lamb. Then the Hebrews must eat roasted lamb quickly, with their belts fastened, their sandals on, and their staffs in their hands. They must be ready to go out from the land of Egypt. And they must keep this day in remembrance forever and ever, for this is the night that I protected them, and passed over their houses." So said the Lord to Moses, who told the people of Israel. And everything the Lord say do, they did.

That night the death angel visited every Egyptian's house, and the firstborn of that family died. Even the firstborn of their cattle and sheep died. Oh, there was a terrible wailing throughout Egypt, a wailing even heard in Pharaoh's house, for his own son was struck dead. But death passed over the homes marked with blood, leaving the Hebrews untouched. My God. My God.

Now, Pharaoh and his people had done seen the power of the Lord and it was terrible. Before rooster crow the next morning, Pharaoh called Moses and Aaron to him. "The Hebrews are free," he said. "Be gone! And if you will, say a prayer for me."

The Egyptians feared for their lives. They were happy to see the Hebrew slaves leave, and gladly heaped clothing, silver ornaments, and gold jewelry upon them. "Take it and go!" they said.

Every man, woman, and child living in Goshen moved with haste, gathering up their b'longings, their cattle, and their sheep. They even now took Joseph's bones with them to bury in their new homeland. The Hebrews were in such a hurry, they didn't wait for their bread to rise, but took it with them unleavened.

All the ancestors of the twelve sons of Israel joined together in one band.

Moses told them, "God has delivered you out of the house of bondage after four hundred and thirty years. You are a free people. Come, let us leave from this place."

"Where are we going?" the people asked.

"We are going to Canaan, the land God promised our ancestors, Abraham, Isaac, and Jacob."

What a day of rejoicing that was! Trumpets sounded. Miriam, Moses' sister, sang praises to the Lord and danced her happiness. A new day had come, and the people were filled with fresh hope.

Moses and Aaron walked at the head of the multitude. During the day they were led by a cloud, and by night they were led by a column of fire. They inched along slowly, mile upon mile, 'cause their numbers were so large. When they came to the Red Sea, they stopped.

Come back to Egyptland, where Pharaoh is just now realizing what he's done. "We have no slaves to work for us," he said. "We have no slaves to build our great cities and monuments or work in our fields."

Pharaoh called for his chariot and his armor. And with his army and six hundred of his best charioteers, he went after the Hebrews, to force them back.

One of the Hebrew lookouts must have seen the great Egyptian army ridin' toward them. I wasn't there, but I imagine that it was a scary sight: all the might of Egypt comin' after them, and comin' fast. The people were terrified. "Look what you've done to us, Moses!" they shouted. "We should have stayed slaves in Egypt rather than die like this."

"You will not die," said Moses calmly. "Don't fret. The Lord has and always will provide for and protect us."

God told Moses to raise his staff over the sea, and Moses obeyed. And behold, the waters divided. Yes, they did. Each side rolled back, and a dry path lay in front of them. Moses shouted over the wind and water, "See the work of the Lord God Almighty."

I s'pose right then the people were amazed and frightened, too. The Hebrews didn't stand around, 'cause they could hear the hooves of Pharaoh's charioteers behind them. They hurried across the Red Sea. But imagine a wall of water on your right, and a wall of water on your left, held back by the power of an unseen God. It was a wonder of wonders, I tell you.

When the last of the Hebrews looked back, they saw Pharaoh and his army ridin' hard, catchin' up. "Look, Moses," the people cried. "The army is upon us. What shall we do?"

Moses raised his staff again, and the walls of towering water came crashin' down on the Egyptians' heads. Their chariots sunk like rocks, and the soldiers, dressed in heavy armor, drowned. Now the Hebrew people were free from bondage. We all know that folks got a way of turnin' things wrongside up. But God will not stand with anything that is wrong. It may take time, but in the end the power of the Lord will bring things to right side up. That was the hard lesson Pharaoh had to learn.

Moses was able now to lead his people into the desert, where they could worship God. But, the Hebrews had lived so long in Egypt, they'd taken on Egypt's ways. For three days, the people were without water, and their thirst made them forget their joy and happiness. "Where is the promised land?" they cried to Moses. "In Egypt there was plenty to drink. We should have stayed there, but instead, we done followed you here to die."

Moses couldn't believe the people had so little faith. He shook his head. "You still don't understand. The Lord has and always will provide and protect us. You will see."

And God showed Moses where there was plenty of water, and for a while the people stood satisfied. God's cloud continued to lead the Hebrews farther into the desert. But soon, there was no food, and their empty stomachs rumbled with hunger. They cried out again, "Look what you've done to us, Moses. We should have stayed in Egypt. We will starve to death on account of you."

"Do not worry," said Moses.

The next morning the people found manna that had fallen from Heaven. To their wonder and surprise, it tasted like bread. And come every morning from then on there was always manna—enough for everybody to eat their fill. The Hebrews were never hungry, 'cause God provided.

God's cloud led the Hebrews even farther into the desert, where they came to Mount Sinai. Moses left the people and went up into the mountains to talk with the Lord. And that is where God gave Moses ten laws, or commandments, for the people to live by:

DO NOT HAVE ANY OTHER GODS BUT THE ONE GOD.

MAKE NO IDOLS OR GRAVEN IMAGES OF FALSE GODS.

DO NOT TAKE THE LORD'S NAME IN VAIN.

REMEMBER THE SABBATH DAY AND KEEP IT HOLY.

HONOR THY FATHER AND THY MOTHER.

DO NOT KILL.

DO NOT COMMIT ADULTERY.

DO NOT STEAL.

DO NOT SPEAK FALSEHOODS AGAINST YOUR NEIGHBOR.

DO NOT COVET OR BE JEALOUS OF ANYTHING THAT
   BELONGS TO YOUR NEIGHBOR.

Another way of saying all this is, if you love God first and with all your heart, mind, and soul, and if you love your neighbor as yourself, then you will honor the laws that were given to Moses.

Come with me back down the mountain to see what the people were doing. While Moses was on the mount, the Hebrews were going to seed, runnin' wild and undisciplined.

Hear what I mean. With their leader gone so long, one or two began to grumble, saying, "Moses done forgot 'bout us."

Someone else took it up, saying, "Moses might be dead."

"We were better off in Egypt," added another.

One rebel say that if they returned with an Egyptian idol in front of them, Pharaoh would be pleased and would welcome them back.

So the Hebrews gathered all the golden jewelry the Egyptians had given them, and forced Aaron to melt it down, then fashion a golden cow. Po' Aaron didn't want to make the idol, but he feared what the people might do to him if he refused.

There in the desert, God's chosen people, the selfsame ones who had been saved from Pharaoh's army, bowed down to a golden idol. They sang before it and danced 'round it. Oh, how they shamed themselves mightily in the sight of God.

Back up on the mountain, God say, "Go down, Moses. Thy people have done a terrible thing. They have made an idol, and for this, I will kill them all."

Moses begged God to be merciful. "Remember the love you showed Abraham and Sarah. Please forgive their descendants now." And once again, the Lord showed mercy for Moses' sake.

Moses came down out of the mountain, carrying the tablets with the Ten Commandments written on them. His face shone with the light of the living Lord, but he was also furious. Moses was so angry, he hurled the stone tablets to the ground and they broke.

Then he took the golden cow the Hebrews had made and burned it.

Now Moses cried out to his people, "Those who are for the Lord, come stand by me." And those who did not come to stand by Moses were killed by those who did—completely destroyed.

The story goes on to say that Moses had the people build a box to hold the Ten Commandments—a very special ark. Then once again the Hebrews set off on their journey, carrying the ark before them.

But in time, the people grew restless and miserable again and they went to complaining. Say, "We tired of eating manna. We want meat."

"These are the most ungrateful people!" said God. "They don't deserve

Moses' face shone with the light of the living Lord

my love and care." But once more, Moses asked God to forgive them. Behold, there appeared birds for them to hunt and eat. And for a while, everybody was content.

At last, the Israelites came near Canaan, the land God had promised Abraham so long ago. But while the Hebrews had been living in Egypt, others had come to live in Canaan. Moses sent twelve men—one from each tribe— to spy out the land and the strength of the people. When they came back, they cried out, "These men of Canaan are fierce. They could easily kill us."

Two men, Joshua and Caleb, were not afraid 'cause they knew they had the strength of the Lord on their side. "God has and always will protect and provide for us."

But others didn't have that faith. "Look at what has happened now, Moses," said the people. "We have no home. We should have stayed in Egypt."

Again, God heard the Israelites' complaining. "Won't these people ever learn?" said God angrily. "I will kill them all and raise up a new nation."

The Hebrews didn't have shackles on their hands and legs anymore. They were a free people. Trouble is, they still thought like slaves. Moses begged and pleaded for God to forgive his people. But this time God would not relent. "I will keep the promise I made to Abraham, Isaac, and Jacob. But these people will not see Canaan. No. They must all die out here in the desert. Their children will go into the promised land, and so will Joshua and Caleb 'cause they b'lieved."

So for forty long years the Hebrews lived in the desert, movin' from one place to another, never settlin' anywhere for very long. Then one day, God took Moses high upon Mount Nebo, and there showed him the land of Canaan. "This is the place that I promised to Abraham, Isaac, and Jacob," God told him. "I wanted you to see Canaan, Moses, but you will not go there."

Moses had to feel sad. He'd come all that way and now he would never cross over into the promised land. But he had to feel good 'bout the new generation of Hebrews he had led through the wilderness. There they were, standin' in the clear light of God's word. All the former slaves had died out, and their children and grandchildren had become a proud people whose faith had made them strong. Moses had taught them well, saying, "Hear, O, Israel, the Lord our God, the Lord is one. You shall love God with all your heart, with all your soul, and with all your might. I command you to let these words flow from your heart when you say them in your lying down time, your rising up time, and when you teach them to your children."

As Moses looked down on his people gathered at the Jordan River, he knew this generation was truly free and ready to claim the promised land. God had brought their mothers and fathers out of bondage 'cause the Lord did not hold with slavery of the mind, the body, or the soul.

Now think on this. God broke the chains of the Hebrews in Egyptland. Should we expect any less for ourselves? I know that the Great God of all Creation will not hold with wrong, never mind those who say otherwise. I will stop here, for this story has no end.

Your God Is My God

RUTH AND NAOMI

The Book of Ruth

I always called my mother's close lady friends "aunt," even though we weren't kin. I was especially fond of Aunt Passy because she acted toward me more like a grandmother than a friend of the family. I visited her regularly at Mr. Rem Tate's plantation, where she was a slave. She was teaching me how to weave baskets made of the sweet grass that grew in the lowlands. As we built them, round after round, she liked to talk about her daughter, Rudine, whom she had not seen in many years.

"I remember the day my child come into this world, feet first and screamin'," she told me. "Her real mama lived just long 'nough to name her Rudine and ask me to see after her. I did more'n that. I loved that li'l baby girl and raised her like she was my own flesh and blood."

One day when I went to the Tates' place, they told me Aunt Passy had been freed. I wanted to be happy about the news, but I couldn't be. The truth was that Mr. Tate had let Aunt Passy go because she was old and no more use

to him in the fields. Figuring it was cheaper to free her than to feed her, he'd just turned her out.

Dear, sweet Aunt Passy had nothing except what was on her back—no work, no money, no family. Mama and Papa made room for her in our house until she could make plans for the future. But I wondered what that future held. Thinking about how she'd been treated made me mad. Thinking about how lonely she would be without any true family made me sad.

I was so moved by these feelings, I hugged Aunt Passy around the neck and cried, "Oh, what's gon' happen to you?"

"I be free," she whispered, gently wiping away my tears, "and freedom gives me hope."

"Hope," I learned from Aunt Passy, is a wonderful word. It can transform you into a different person. Aunt Passy didn't fold up and die, as we'd all expected. Freedom had given her something to live for—the hope that she'd reunite with her daughter, Mis Rudine.

With Papa's help, Aunt Passy got the Brown Fellowship Society, an organization of freemen of color in Charleston, to start a search for her daughter. Last word, she was now a freed woman, living in Philadelphia. As the months passed, I began to doubt if they'd ever find her. And even if they did, would she come to Charleston?

Most free blacks who left South Carolina never came back. Papa said there were so many laws in these parts against them, it was almost impossible for them to travel about. And even when they did, there was the chance that they might be captured and sold into slavery. I wondered would Mis Rudine care enough to risk her freedom to see about a woman who wasn't her real mother?

Aunt Passy went on day after day, making and selling winnowing baskets and keeping her hope fresh by telling me more stories about her beloved Rudine.

"It's been near 'bout ten years since I seen my daughter," Aunt Passy said, her hands busy weaving the long strips of sweet grass. "You know, Mr. Tate gave her to his daughter Mary Louise as a wedding present. They went off to live in Philadelphia. When Mary Louise died a few months after they got there, her husband freed Rudine. I lost touch with my precious girl after that, but I'm gon' see her again 'fore I leave this world. God's gon' give me that." I wondered how Aunt Passy could be so sure.

Then one day, after nearly a year of waiting, good news came from a sailor who was a member of the Free African Society up in Philadelphia. They'd found Mis Rudine. The plan was, they were going to sneak her into Charleston to see Aunt Passy. She was due to arrive on the *Chelsea* within the month.

I don't know if we rejoiced more on that day or the day Mis Rudine actually walked into our house. Even though her daughter was disguised as a sailor, Aunt Passy immediately recognized her. She was purely overcome, laughing and crying at the same time. "I knew you'd come," she said. "I can die now in peace having done seen my baby one more time."

"No, Mama," said Mis Rudine. "You're coming back with me to Philadelphia. I've made all the arrangements."

As the two of them sat beside each other, talking and making plans, I felt a little guilty for having doubted Mis Rudine. I reached out and took my own mother's hand. She gave it a gentle squeeze.

"They are remarkable women—genuinely devoted to each other," Mama said quietly.

"They remind me of Ruth and Naomi," Papa said.

And sitting together in the cool of the evening, as the katydids sang, Papa told me about two other remarkable women who loved each other dearly.

Come with me to the way back time after Moses had died. Joshua had become the leader of the Israelites and the commander of their army. Joshua fit the battle of Jericho, and the Israelites took over Canaan, the place God had promised Abraham, Isaac, and Jacob. The land was divided up 'tween the twelve tribes of Israel, the ancestors of the twelve sons of Jacob. 'Stead of a king, the Israelites were ruled by judges who were s'posed to govern them according to the laws of Moses.

It was during that time that a terrible famine shadowed the land of Canaan. No rains fell, and the earth dried up. So did the wells. The crops failed. The cattle and sheep died. And the men of Israel cried out:

"Dear God in Heaven,
We know how to plow;
We know how to sow;
We know how to reap and thresh.
But we have no crops to harvest."

In Canaan's city of Bethlehem there lived a man named Elimelech. He and his family were suffering same as all the other Israelites. His crops had failed year after year. His flocks were dying off, lamb by lamb. His family went to bed hungry. So Elimelech said to his wife, Naomi, "Come, let us take our sons and move to a new land where there is no famine."

Now, Naomi was like most of us. She didn't want to leave the only home she'd ever known. She'd lived in Bethlehem all her life. Her family and friends were there. "We won't tarry long," said Elimelech. "We'll return when the hard times done passed."

Since Naomi loved and trusted her husband, she set out for a new land with him, her sons, Mahlon and Chilion, and what few mules, horses, camels, cattle, donkeys, and sheep were left.

Oh, that had to be a sad day for Naomi—leavin' her kin and goin' to a

Elimelech's flocks were dying off, lamb by lamb

place she didn't know nothing 'bout. But Naomi trusted in the one God. Say, "The Lord God is good as well as great," she said.

Elimelech and Naomi traveled a long and winding path, going toward the east. Every morning they walked toward the rising sun; every night the sun set at their backs. They went over mountains and down through the wilderness, moving slow but steady-like, day by day, ever moving east. And at last, they came to the land of Moab.

The Moabites' land was full of plenty. They had more than enough of everything good to eat and drink. Their pastures were green, and their soil was rich. The Moabite men say:

"We plow and sow.

We reap and thresh.

We praise our gods for the harvest."

This troubled Naomi's heart and mind and touched her very soul. The Moabites worshipped gods made of stone and wood. They didn't b'lieve in the God of Abraham, Isaac, Jacob, and Moses. But Naomi did. "Jehovah is the true God," she said. Then she made a promise to the Lord. "I will live here in Moab, but I will honor you always." And Naomi loved the Lord and honored the laws of Moses as they had been given to him on Mount Sinai long ago.

Times passed—some good, some bad—and the family went right on livin'. Naomi and Elimelech made peace with their new home, and there was little or no talk 'bout going back home to Bethlehem. Then without warning, Elimelech up and died. Right now. Po' Naomi was natural-born hurt. You know she was. But in time the sadness became less burdensome. Say she still had two sons. "I am happy to have you, my dear boys," she told them.

More times passed—some good, some bad—but it all evened out. Now Naomi's son Mahlon fell in love with a beautiful Moabite girl named Ruth, and they married. Naomi's son Chilion fell in love, too, and married a

Moabite named Orpah. Naomi counted herself blessed to have two strong sons and two lovely daughters-in-law. "I am happy to have you all," she said.

Through all these changes and all this passing of time, Naomi never, not once, forgot her promise. She and her family had prospered in Moab, but she remained faithful to the one true God, who was good as well as great.

"Since Jehovah is your God, Jehovah is my God, too," Ruth told Naomi.

"Jehovah is my God, too," said Orpah.

This pleased Naomi and she came to love her daughters-in-law very, very much.

It happened that a great tragedy befell the family. Both Mahlon and Chilion took ill and died. This had to be Naomi's lowest hour, both of her own boys dead. Still, her faith held strong. She looked at her daughters-in-law, saying, "I have no husband, no sons, no chance of any more children. Even so, God is good as well as great. I have you."

Then word came to Naomi that things had changed back home in the land of Israel. Word tell, the men of Israel could be heard shouting:

"Great God, Jehovah!

We plow and sow;

We reap and thresh;

God blesses our bountiful harvest."

When Naomi heard this, she longed to go home—home to the land of her father and mother. But she had been gone so long, she'd grown old and tired. She had no husband and no sons to see after her. Naomi had lost everything. Still, she was determined.

Since Ruth and Orpah couldn't sway Naomi, they decided to go 'long with her. But Naomi told them, "Stay here, 'mongst your people." Still, the women say, "We will all go together."

Straightaway, the three of them packed up what little they owned and set out for Bethlehem, moving west, always west. The road was crooked. The ruts in the path made the women stumble, and the thorny bushes scratched their ankles. The sun beat down on their po' heads, and sweat ran down their faces. But they huddled together, helping one another, and in this way they inched along.

A few days out, Naomi turned to her daughters-in-law. "Go back," she cried. "I'm old. I got nothing to offer you in Bethlehem. Please. I love you both, but it would be best for you to go on home."

But neither one was willing to leave Naomi. They told her they loved her and wanted to stay with her.

Naomi would not let it rest. "You must listen," she insisted. "I have no more sons for you to marry. No money. No land. No flocks. Nothing!"

Orpah studied on it. Then sadly she hugged Ruth and Naomi and turned back toward Moab, her family, and the gods she once worshipped.

Ruth, too, listened to all of Naomi's protests. At last she told her mother-in-law, say, "I will not leave you. Wherever you go, I will go. Your people will be my people. Your God will be my God. I want to live and die wherever you are."

Naomi knew then that Ruth could not be made to go back. Together the women traveled forward, over mountains, through wilderness and past dry lands. At last they came to Bethlehem.

God blessed Naomi for her loving kindness and faithfulness with a long and happy life. And God blessed Ruth for her loyalty. Ruth married Naomi's kinsman, Boaz, and they were the parents of Obed, who was the father of Jesse, who was the father of King David. God is great as well as good. On that point, I give my final word.

Then sadly Orpah hugged Ruth

To Slay a Giant

DAVID AND

GOLIATH

I Samuel: 8, 9, 15, 16, 17

I tremble slightly whenever I recall that late summer day in September of 1812, when Peter Willy asked me to help him run away.

After delivering a hat to one of Mama's customers over on Calhoun Street, I decided to take a roundabout way home, zigzagging up one street and down the other. While heading down St. Philip Street, I came to the grand Armstrong house, where T. J. Armstrong lived, one of the wealthiest and most powerful merchants in all of Charleston. Peter Willy, a slave of his, was working on the front lawn.

"Morning, Charlotte," he said, looking to see if there was anybody around who could overhear our conversation. "You the one I been waitin' for. You're perfect!"

"Me?" I answered, wondering what on earth Peter Willy might mean. Secretly, I thought he was the most handsome young man around, with his broad shoulders and strong hands. But he was sixteen, and I was just twelve. He'd hardly even noticed me before.

"I'm gettin' sold," he whispered, speaking quickly. "Come Friday, I'm gon' to be put on the block."

I was shocked and bewildered. The memory of losing my friend Cree washed over me like a big wave, and I shouted out without thinking, "They can't do that to me—to you, I mean."

Peter Willy put his finger over my mouth and looked me square in the face. "Shhhh! I aine got time to do no lots of talkin', but I aim to be far 'way from this place 'fore Friday. And I needs you to help me. Can I depend on you to help me?"

Without thinking about the consequences, I committed myself on the spot with a promise.

It was only later, in the quiet of my sleeping loft, that I became frightened. What had I gotten myself into? Peter Willy's master was a very powerful man. If we got caught, he could swat us like mosquitoes. Why hadn't I remembered how dangerous it was to aid a runaway?

I spent two days worrying and wondering what Peter Willy might ask me to do. My imagination conjured up terrible images.

At last the day came.

Every Thursday Peter Willy delivered receipts to Mr. Armstrong's bookkeeper. After making the delivery that day, he met me at Concord Street on the porch of an abandoned mansion. The owners were away for the summer. The church bells rang the three hour. "I'm ever grateful that you came," he said. I wondered could he hear my heart beating, see the fear in my face?

"We aine got much time," he said, urgency filling his voice.

I listened in absolute amazement as he detailed his escape route. Peter Willy was going to ship himself to the home of a free black in Philadelphia!

He stepped inside a large wooden box he had constructed, complete with several small holes for air. Inside, Peter Willy had stored dried meat and water, and a small hand ax. "I hired a shipping company to pick up the box and load it on the *Pelican*, one of Massa's own ships, and I charged it to his account," he explained. He'd have to be in that box for six days or more while the merchant ship made its way to Philadelphia. But once there, he'd climb out of the box a freeman. "They think I'se a table—being sent north," he told me.

Peter Willy seemed to have thought of everything. Strange as it was, the plan sounded like it might work. "What you want me to do?" I asked.

"There was one thing I couldn't figure out how to do for myself," he said. "I need you to lock me inside so nobody can open the box."

"Is that all?"

He nodded.

So many more questions crowded my mind, but all I could think to say was, "You so brave. I'm gon' always remember you."

"You always be right here," he said, pointing to his heart. "Charlotte, you have helped slay the giant." And with a quick smile, Peter Willy sat down in the box and pulled the lid shut.

Now all I had to do was push the padlock until I heard it click. Just in time, too, because I heard footsteps drawing near.

Slipping to the side of the mansion, I watched as two men approached, picked up the box, and heaved it onto their shoulders. Grumbling, they carried it away. It was the last I ever saw of Peter Willy.

Soon after, Papa told me that Mr. Armstrong put out a reward for the boy's capture and return. But we heard from sailors that upon reaching his destination, Peter Willy had hacked his way out of the box and burst forth, a freeman. He was mighty stiff and powerful hungry, but none the worse for all he'd been through. In my own small way I celebrated in his victory,

imagining myself there with him, listening to his story and applauding his triumphant escape.

Finally I got the nerve to tell Mama and Papa about my involvement. Right away Mama declared me a rebel and forbade me ever to do such a thing again. Papa scolded me, too. But there was the hint of a smile in his eyes, and I knew he wasn't nearly as mad as he put on.

"Papa," I asked boldly, "Peter Willy say I had helped him slay the giant. What giant do you s'ppose he was talking 'bout?"

"Ah," Papa began with a forgiving wink. "I 'spect he was talking 'bout his massa. To a slave, his mas' seems like an undefeatable giant, a Goliath of sorts. As you done come to know, to slay a giant you got to have faith in God and confidence in yo'self—just like David."

"Was David as scared as me, I wonder?"

"I reckon he had cause to be scared," he said, "but like a proverb reminds us: 'Whoso putteth his trust in the Lord shall be safe.'"

As darkness cocooned us within our house, Papa lit a candle, then began the story of a brave shepherd boy who put his trust in God.

In my mind, God is like a patient, protecting father, a kind and forgiving mother, and a generous and loving brother or sister. But sometimes God's own children must seem like strangers. I'm sure God didn't recognize the judges who ruled the Israelites, for they fell headlong into corruption. Now the Israelites figured they knew how to fix it. "Having a king will be better than having judges," they said.

Samuel was a prophet, one of God's messengers. He heard the people's words and prayed for God's guidance. "Oh Lord," he asked. "Why don't the Israelites understand that you are the only king they need?"

"Samuel," God said, "make sure they are warned 'bout the ways of an earthly king."

Samuel tried to show the Israelites the trouble they was brewing. "Don't you know that a king will take your sons to be in his army? A king will take the women among you and make them be cooks and bakers and such. A king will take a tenth of all your harvests as taxes. The very king you are beggin' so for today you will want to be rid of tomorrow."

"No we won't," shouted the people.

So God told Samuel, "Let it be. Give them what they want."

That is how Saul, from the tribe of Benjamin, became the first king of Israel. But sorry to say, Saul's pride got him in trouble, and he ended up out of favor with God. Samuel delivered God's message to Saul. "The Lord has turned away from you," he said, and then he left and saw Saul no more. Though still the king, Saul was a changed man, troubled in his heart and mind. But that's another story.

Samuel traveled to the small town of Bethlehem, where a man named Jesse lived. Remember, Jesse was the son of Obed, who was the son of Ruth, who was the daughter-in-law of Naomi. Jesse had many fine sons, and Samuel knew that one of them had been chosen by God to follow Saul as the next king of Israel—but he didn't know just which one.

When Samuel saw Jesse's oldest son, he thought, This must be the one, the one God has chosen. Look how tall and strong and handsome he is.

The Lord told Samuel to beware. "Do not be misled by outward appearances, for I do not see as you do. This young man may be strong, but what is in his heart? No, this is not the one."

Samuel saw the next son. I am sure this must be the one, thought Samuel. But God say not so.

Jesse was proud of his sons and gladly showed them off to Samuel. But none was God's choice. "Do you have another son?" Samuel asked Jesse.

"Yes. My youngest son is David. He is away herding sheep. I will send for him."

When Samuel saw David, the prophet got an instant understanding. This was the one, the one the Almighty had chosen. Samuel anointed the shepherd boy by pouring oil on his head, and the spirit of the Lord favored David and was with him from that day on.

David didn't let all that ceremony turn his head, though. He went back to tending his father's sheep. To soothe his flock and pass the long, lonely hours, David made up beautiful psalms—songs of praise. I imagine I can hear him playing his harp and singing joyfully,

> "The Lord is my shepherd; I shall not want.
>
> He maketh me to lie down in green pastures:
>
> he leadeth me beside the still waters.
>
> He restoreth my soul:
>
> he leadeth me in the paths of righteousness
>
>   for his name's sake."

David knew that the lion and the wolf were always lurkin' outside the circle of light; danger and death were always one mistake away. But he took comfort in knowin' God was a constant companion. I imagine I can hear his voice floatin' on the night currents, saying steadfastly,

> "Yea, though I walk through the valley of
>
>   the shadow of death,
>
> I will fear no evil: for thou art with me;
>
> thy rod and thy staff they comfort me."

David went back to tending his father's sheep

No doubt David, in his solitude under the open sky, often told God how he felt. Can't you hear those beautiful words as David would have said them, long ago, on a faraway hillside:

"Thou preparest a table before me in the
    presence of mine enemies:
thou anointest my head with oil;
my cup runneth over.
Surely goodness and mercy shall follow me
    all the days of my life:
and I will dwell in the house of the Lord
    for ever."

Now it came to pass that the Israelites went to war with the Philistines. King Saul and his army camped on one hill, the Philistine army camped on the opposite one. The two armies faced each other, both ready for battle.

The Philistines had a soldier named Goliath, who was a giant, standing six-seven-eight-nine feet tall. They sent him out to talk. The very ground shook 'neath his footfall. "Bring forth your best soldier. I will fight him," he shouted. "If he kills me, the Philistines will serve the Israelites. If I kill him, the Israelites will serve the Philistines."

But Goliath was so big, so strong, and so ugly, nobody in King Saul's army wanted to face him. King Saul asked round, hoping to find one warrior who would take up the sword. It wasn't that Saul's men were cowardly. Goliath was just so big, nobody felt like they had a chance.

The ground shook, and everybody knew Goliath was coming out to challenge them again. "Send your best soldier and I will fight him," he bellowed like a bull. Every day the giant made the same offer. And every day Saul's men refused it.

Then one day Jesse said to David, who had stayed behind to tend the sheep, "Take food to your brothers at the army camp." David hurried to obey his father.

The shepherd boy arrived at the camp long 'bout when Goliath was coming out on the hill. He was the biggest, meanest-looking somebody David had ever seen. "Send your best soldier and I will fight him," Goliath growled.

David went to King Saul. "Send me. I will fight Goliath," he said, filled with confidence.

Saul was amazed. Here was a boy ready to fight the giant that all of his soldiers were 'fraid to face. "No," Saul said. "You are too young, too small. Goliath is a giant and a mighty soldier."

But David answered, "God has protected me before, and God will protect me now." Maybe he was thinking 'bout one of his psalms to bolster his courage: *I will lift up mine eyes unto the hills from whence cometh my help. My help cometh from the Lord which made heaven and earth.*

Saul agreed when he saw how determined David was, but he insisted that the boy wear the king's own armor. But Saul's armor was heavy and much too big for young David. The shepherd boy took it off, saying, "I will take my sling and my staff. That is all I needed when God helped me fight a lion and a bear. God is with me now."

When Goliath saw David, he roared with laughter. The ground shook as he walked toward the small warrior. "Do you think I'm a dog you can fight with sticks?" the giant snarled.

"God will defeat you this day," said David, picking up five smooth river stones. He put a stone in his sling.

'Round and 'round David swung the sling over his head. In his mind he must have been calling upon the Lord for courage:

"For, I will not trust in my bow,
neither shall my sword save me.

But thou hast saved us from our enemies,
and hast put them to shame that hated us.
In God we boast all the day long,
and praise thy name for ever."

The boy took careful aim and rushed toward the giant. He let the stone fly. *Swooooooooh!* It hit Goliath square in the middle of his forehead.

Goliath shook from head to toe, blinked his eyes, and keeled over like a rootless tree. Quickly, David rushed for a sword and chopped off the giant's head.

The Philistines scattered like snakes fleeing from fire when they saw that a mere boy had defeated the best among them.

Word spread quickly that David had killed the Philistine giant. The Israelites loved him and sang songs 'bout him. But David gave God the glory.

David the shepherd boy was a natural-born leader who would go on to become one of the greatest kings of Israel. During his long and glorious life, he had to slay many giants that loomed tall in the form of big, big troubles and great mistakes. How did he do it? Hear King David's voice, singing to us from the ages:

"Blessed is the man that walketh not in the
   counsel of the ungodly,
nor standeth in the way of sinners,
nor sitteth in the seat of the scornful.
But his delight is in the law of the Lord;
and in his law doth he mediate day and night.
And he shall be like a tree, planted by
   the river water,
that bringeth forth his fruit in his season;
his leaf also shall not wither;
and whatsoever he doeth shall prosper . . .
the way of the ungodly shall perish."

The boy took careful aim

What Do You Pray For?

THE WISDOM OF SOLOMON

1 Kings 3: 5–9

During the summer when the heat of the anvil and the heat of the sun were equally hot, Papa and his helpers always took a break. All of my friends gathered at that time, too, just to hear him talk.

Papa loved an interesting discussion and always posed questions that would spark us. One day he asked, "What do you ask from God when you pray?"

"I ask for a good ship and a decent captain," said Alonzo, a Portuguese lad whose skin was as dark as my own. Whenever his ship was in port, he worked with Papa at the forge.

"I ask for freedom," said Josie, a slave girl whose mistress had sent her to Mama to learn how to sew.

Sad-eyed Jesse said, "I want to see my dear mama again."

Mama, who was sitting nearby, allowed that she wanted good health for herself and her family. Everybody agreed that hers was a mother's true prayer.

When all the others had answered, Papa turned to me. "And what do you pray for, Charlotte?"

Nobody had spoken about great wealth. "Is it wrong to pray for riches?" I asked.

"Who would pray to be poor? But there is a wise saying that reminds us that worldly possessions can grow wings like an eagle and fly away."

"What do you pray for, Brother Jefferies?" Jesse asked.

I wondered myself what Papa's answer would be. "First, I thank God for my blessings, then I ask for the same thing Solomon did."

"Tell us what it was."

In the shade of the large live oak out behind the forge Papa began the story of Solomon the King.

※

Think of being told by the Great God Almighty that you could have anything you wanted. Wouldn't that be a wonderful thing? Or would it? King Solomon was given such a choice.

According to God's plan, when King David died, his son Solomon became king of Israel. The Lord visited Solomon in a dream, saying, "Whatever you want I will give it to you. All you have to do is ask."

Now Solomon didn't want to make a hasty decision, so he took time to study on all the possibilities.

Should I ask for riches? Solomon wondered. With gold I could build a great palace that would be the envy of all other kings. But he knew that worldly goods last only a little while. Should I ask for strength and power? With a large army I could crush my enemies. Or should I ask for good health and a long life—then I could enjoy my children and my grandchildren. Solomon weighed all those thoughts in his mind. Wealth. Fame. Health. Long life. What would it be?

At last, Solomon decided not to ask for any of these things. In a prayer of thanksgiving, he praised the Lord for all the blessings he already had received. Then Solomon said with a humble heart, "Lord, you have made me king. All I ask is you please give me the wisdom to rule yo' people well."

God took joy in Solomon's answer. "As you have asked, I will give you a wise and understanding heart. I will also give you all those things that you did not ask for—riches, power, health. No other king will equal you."

Solomon woke from his dream and he was deeply moved. He praised God again for the blessing.

It wasn't long 'fore Solomon's wisdom was put to a real test.

Two women came to him and bowed ever so humble-like. Each one cried out for justice. The first woman say, "Dearest King, this woman and I live in the same house. I had a baby, born strong and healthy. She gave birth to a lifeless baby three days later. While I slept she put her dead baby in my arms and took my living baby to be her own. Please, I want my child back."

Solomon listened to the second woman's story. It was just as believable. "The living baby is mine," she pleaded real pitiful-like. "The dead one is hers. Now she wants to steal my child. I won't let her have him."

The great king studied on what the women had said—looking into their eyes, hoping to find some proof of their honesty. Both women seemed so sincere, so certain. How could he tell who the real mother was?

"I see what needs to be done," he said at last. "Get me a sword and I will cut the child in two. Each one will have her half. That is fair."

"Good," said the second woman. "Let it be so. Neither she nor I will have the baby."

"No, no!" the first woman begged. "Please, give her the baby, instead. Don't harm him, Great King."

Solomon took the baby and placed it in the first woman's arms. "You are the real mother," he said, "because you were willing to give him up to save his life. Go in peace."

"Get me a sword," said Solomon.

From that day on, Solomon became known far and wide as Solomon the Wise. And God showered him with honor and riches, and Solomon used the fortune to build a great temple in Jerusalem where the children of Israel could worship the Lord.

If you are blessed with true wisdom, you will have one of the greatest gifts God has to offer. For when money is spent, when food spoils, when clothing is worn out, when houses crumble, and ships sink, wisdom will last from ever to ever.

No Greater Love

QUEEN ESTHER

The Book of Esther

*O*ne morning, when it was day clean, Papa sent me to pick up Mama at the Murphys' house. She had helped deliver their new baby the night before. As I turned the corner onto Broad Street, I smelled smoke and heard the fire bells ringing. People were running toward Matthew Delaney's building. It was located near the Exchange Building and used as a holding place where African captives were chained up until they were auctioned at the slave market. The conditions were so awful inside, most of us called it "the Dungeon." What was going to happen to the people held there? I wondered. After I'd helped Peter Willy escape, Mama and Papa had warned me never to put myself in harm's way. But I just had to find out.

Smoke billowed from the Dungeon's roof, and flames leaped out of the broken windows. Several lines of volunteers quickly passed buckets of water along, trying to contain the fire, but their efforts were hopeless. I slid off our horse, Blackberry, tied him to a hitching rail, and pushed through the crowd.

Boldly, I approached Mr. Delaney himself. "What about the people inside, sir?" I asked desperately. "Did they get out?"

"I've lost everything," was his only reply.

I didn't feel one bit sorry for him or that the Dungeon was burning down, but I dreaded seeing the captives die in the process. "Can't you do something?" I asked. Mr. Delaney shook his head.

"Those are human beings in there, not sacks of flour or beans. Can't you hear their screams for help?" said Mis Liza Moreau, who was coming toward Mr. Delaney, walking fast and with a purpose. She was one of Mama's best customers and one of the most fashionable ladies in Charleston society.

"Why, Mis Moreau, there's nothing I can do."

"Then will you take fifty dollars for them?" she said, opening her purse.

What could she possibly be thinking, I wondered, wanting to buy a bunch of soon to be dead slaves?

Straightaway Mr. Delaney accepted the deal. As soon as he took the money, Mis Moreau demanded the keys to the leg shackles that bound the slaves one to the other.

A piece of the roof caved in, and choking smoke drove some of the fire-fighters back. We could hear the horrible moaning and pleading from inside. Quickly Mis Moreau poured a bucket of water over her hair. Why, she was going to go in there, I realized, and the water was to keep her hair from catching fire. When she wet her clothing, Mr. Delaney also knew what she was about to do. He grabbed her arm, saying, "I cannot stand by and allow a white woman to endanger her life for a bunch of wild, black heathens."

"Take your hand away," Mis Moreau replied angrily, her eyes narrowing to slits. "I *am* one of those wild, black heathens. They are my people, and I will not see them die this way!" She turned to the crowd. "Who will help me?" And without hesitation, she ran into the burning building.

I started to follow, inspired by Mis Moreau's words and actions, but strong hands held me back. "Charlotte Jefferies, what are you doing here?"

It was Papa. He had come in answer to the fire bells that were ringing all over Charleston. He ordered me to go stand by Blackberry. Then he hurried to help Mis Moreau. When other people of color saw their bravery, they joined in the rescue, too, going into the burning building and leading the captives to safety. Not one person perished, either—not one—even though the Dungeon was totally destroyed.

We were never to see Mis Moreau again. Once the truth that she had been passing for white was out, her life was in real danger. She secretly left Charleston just ahead of a tar-and-feathering mob—but not before she'd taken care of the captives she'd saved. Mis Moreau had sold the slaves to a well-known antislavery lawyer who freed them all, just as she wanted.

To this day, I still think about Mis Moreau and the brave thing she did. During the years that followed, we heard all manner of rumors about her— that she was living a life of privilege in Paris; that she had returned to where she'd been born in Haiti and served as a spy for the rebels in the war against slavery there, and more. Wherever she was, I imagined myself by her side taking a stand, right in the thick of things.

Papa was upset with me for being at the fire that day, and Mama would have probably switched my legs if she'd seen me, but I was too excited to worry about that. "Mis Moreau is a brave, brave woman," I said to Papa as he put me on Blackberry.

"She has the spirit of Queen Esther, all right!"

"Who was Queen Esther?" I wanted to know.

Papa climbed up behind me. "She was smart, beautiful, and bold," he said, turning Blackberry toward Broad Street. And with the smell of smoke still pungent in the air, Papa told me her story.

—⁓⁓⁓—

Before Esther was a queen, she was a captive, living in a foreign land. She and her people had been defeated after years of civil war and fighting. The cause of those wars go back to when Solomon was king of Israel.

Remember, Solomon was known for being wise. Well, his wisdom failed him when it came to women. Here's what I mean. He married women from the four corners of the earth and gave them anything—no, everything—they wanted. He even let them worship their own gods and built altars for them.

For this, God was angry and sent word through a prophet, saying, "Solomon, I'm gon' tear your kingdom apart. But for the love of David I will not do so 'fore you die."

Solomon ruled for forty golden years, and the Hebrew nation was prosperous and peaceful. When he died, though, the twelve tribes of Israel commenced to fightin' 'mongst themselves. They couldn't decide who was to be their next king.

Finally, the tribes of Judah and Benjamin went to the southern part of the country and set up the Kingdom of Judah. They had their own king. The other ten tribes formed the Kingdom of Israel in the northern part of the country. And they had their own king.

Turned out that both were wicked men. In fact, Judah and Israel were ruled by a whole chain of wicked kings. And over time their endless fighting weakened their defenses and made it easier for outsiders to slip in and defeat both kingdoms.

There came a time when the Jehudites, or Jews of Judah, were took over by the Persians and carried off as prisoners of war. The Jews were then spread throughout the kingdom, where they lived among strangers far, far from home.

Mordecai was a Jew, a Benjaminite, who had been captured and taken from his home in Judah. He lived in the city of Shushan with his cousin Esther, whose parents were dead. Mordecai and Esther loved each other as father and daughter.

King Ahasuerus was lord of the land, and he was worshipped as a god. But Mordecai and his household stayed loyal to God and obeyed the laws of Moses.

Word tell, King Ahasuerus had a pretty wife named Queen Vashti—so pretty, he wanted to show her off in front of his friends. But when he sent for her one night at a huge banquet he was holding, she refused to answer her husband. Say she would not come to him.

The king took great offense and studied on how he could punish the queen. He asked his counselors, who urged him to be severe lest Queen Vashti set a bad example for other women; they didn't want wives disobeyin' husbands all over the kingdom.

King Ahasuerus agreed with his counselors and quit Queen Vashti straightaway—took everything 'way from her, too. Then the king commenced to looking for a new wife.

He had the most beautiful maidens in all the land brought to his palace. Esther was natural-born pretty, and as smart as she was beautiful. She was one of those taken to the king's court. But before Esther went, Mordecai warned her never to let on that she was a Jew. And she took heed.

Every day for near 'bout a year, Mordecai, who was the king's gatekeeper, passed the place where Esther and the other maidens waited for the king to see them. In this way Mordecai kept watch over his charge without raisin' suspicion. He was pleased to learn that Esther was admired by everybody around her . . . but Mordecai never 'llowed that they were kin.

Came the day Esther was taken to King Ahasuerus. When he laid first eye on her, he set the queen's crown on her head—made her his wife, right now. From then on, she was Queen Esther.

Soon after Esther's marriage, Mordecai got wind of a plot to kill the king. He told Queen Esther, who told her husband, making sure Mordecai's name was mentioned. King Ahasuerus caught the men set to kill him and had them hung. He praised Esther, and his love for her grew even stronger. But he forgot to give Mordecai his due.

Now, there was a snake-of-a-man in the king's service by the name of Haman. And like a lot of wicked people often do, he won the king's favor and was raised to second in command over the whole kingdom. Mean times were in store for the Jews—'specially po' Mordecai.

Everybody feared Haman and with good reason—he wore his wickedness like a robe of honor and forced folks to bow down when they greeted him. They all did so, not out of respect, but absolute fear. But Mordecai the gatekeeper wouldn't do so. Say, "I bow only to the one true God, the Almighty."

Esther was taken to King Ahasuerus

This didn't set well with Haman, and a terrible hatred rose up in his heart 'gainst Mordecai. On that account Haman turned his hand 'gainst all Jews, promising to destroy every one that was livin' in the kingdom! Oh, what woes befall good people when wrong is in power.

Haman set out to fulfill his terrible plan. He sided up to the king, saying, "There're those living 'mongst us who don't obey the king's laws. If you agree, let me order them to be killed, all of them."

King Ahasuerus believed Haman was acting in good faith, so he took a ring from his finger and gave it to him. "Do with them whatever you please." Now Haman had the authority to carry out the full measure of his wickedness, and nobody—so he thought—could stop him. Under the king's seal, Haman sent word throughout the land ordering that all the Jews were to be put to death.

Say when Mordecai heard 'bout this, he ripped his clothing and poured ashes over his head. "Woe, woe be unto my people and me," he cried.

Meanwhile Esther didn't know what was going on till Mordecai sent a message to her that all the Jews were under the decree of death. He was asking for her help. Could she prevent them from being slaughtered?

Esther had to help, but her plan was risky. In that country, if anybody, even the queen, went before the king without his permission, he or she would be put to death. That is, unless the king held out his golden scepter to say it was all right. Esther sent word to Mordecai to gather up all the Jews and fast for three days and nights—neither eat nor drink. "I will fast, too. And then I will go before the king on your behalf," she said. "If I die, so be it."

Brave Queen Esther approached the king. One word, and he could have had her killed. But when he saw her, he held out his golden scepter. "What do you want, my queen? I will give you whatever it is, up to half of my kingdom."

"If the king's heart is open, let him hear my request at dinner tonight," she said. "Please come, and bring Haman with you."

The king gladly accepted. That evening he and Haman enjoyed the fine feast she had prepared for them.

Once again the king asked, "What can I do for you, dear queen? You may have whatever you ask for up to half of my kingdom." Queen Esther asked only that the king and Haman return the next day for another meal.

Haman was full of himself when he left the queen's chambers. But he grew angry when he saw Mordecai, the one man who would not bow down to him.

When Haman reached his house, he called his wife and friends to him, boasting and bragging 'bout how favored he was. "I was the only one asked to have dinner with the king and queen, and I've even been asked to dine with them again tomorrow."

But Haman couldn't put away his hatred for Mordecai. "None of my wealth and power means anything so long as Mordecai lives," he said. Then he ordered gallows to be built seventy-five feet high. "I will hang Mordecai come morning," he announced.

Meanwhile, King Ahasuerus couldn't sleep. He got up in the middle of the night and, of all things, asked for a reading of the court records. And lo, he was reminded of how Mordecai had saved his life. "Did I do anything to honor this man?" the king asked.

"No, nothing," answered the king's servant.

Come first light, King Ahasuerus asked Haman what ought to be done for a man he wanted to honor. Thinking the king was talkin' 'bout him, Haman commenced to say, "I'd give him a fine robe, a horse, and a crown, and have one of your princes lead him through the streets so all can see how much you think of this man."

"Very well, then," the king told Haman. "Do everything you have said for Mordecai, the gatekeeper."

That made Haman madder than a swamp adder. Haman's wife had warned him that Mordecai would be the cause of his downfall, but before Haman could hatch another wicked scheme, he was called to dinner by the queen's servant.

Queen Esther had a delicious meal prepared for her husband and Haman. There was plenty of everything good to eat and drink. When they were full, King Ahasuerus asked Esther, "Now tell me, dear queen, what is your request?"

Esther began with a plea. "If you care for me, great king, please spare my life and my people's lives, for we are about to be killed because we are Jews."

The king stood up in anger. "Name the person who would kill you."

Esther pointed to Haman. "He, sitting here at my table. Haman has tricked you into believing that my people mean you harm. You have given him the authority to kill all Jews living in your kingdom. But I am a Jew and I beg you to have mercy."

The king loved Esther very much. He was so angry, he ordered Haman to be hung on the same gallows Haman had built for Mordecai. As for Mordecai, he was given Haman's job, his house, and his authority.

But Esther was still concerned about her people. She went to her husband and said, "It is well that my family is safe, but is there something you can do to stop other Jews from being killed? I can't endure the pain of seeing my people slaughtered."

King Ahasuerus shook his head. "In this land," he said sadly, "even I can't stop an order once I have given it. But," he added after studying on it a spell, "there is something else I can do."

The king made a new order, decreeing that the Jews had a right to take up arms and defend themselves. And in this way they were saved from slaughter. Queen Esther was honored by her people—as she still is even to this day.

Queen Esther could have remained silent and let thousands of people die. Instead, she risked her own life to save others. There is nothing braver a person can do.

Esther pointed to Haman

A Change of Heart

THE STORY OF JONAH

The Book of Jonah

When I was thirteen we had one of the worst hurricanes I can remember. But that time stays in my mind for another reason. It was the year I saw a dead man walk among the living again.

Ship crews and passengers connected us to places beyond Charleston by bringing us bits and pieces of stories, ideas, and fresh gossip. Seamen also brought us reports about bad weather coming our way, especially hurricanes that blew in from the Big Water between July and November. Their warning gave us time to prepare for the high winds and crushing hurricane water.

One September Bill and Kinks, two sailors from the *Lady Slipper*, came to a meeting at our house. I overheard them tell Papa that his old ship, the *Gabriel*, had been caught in a squall off the Atlantic coast of Florida and had sunk like a rock. Their own ship had escaped a similar fate by running with full sails ahead of another storm. This same storm was about two days out, heading straight for Charleston.

Papa thanked his friends for the information, then asked, "Any word of Captain Shelby Price?"

"Gone to judgment," said Bill. Papa just nodded.

I wondered how my father's old master had been judged when he stood before his Maker. But there was so much to do to prepare for the storm, I quickly put Captain Price out of my mind.

The next day it was hot and sticky. The low and fast-moving clouds hung heavy over the city like a sour rag. Papa went to pick up whale oil for our lamps while Mama was away getting a few cooking staples. I was left at home to gather vegetables from our garden.

Suddenly I felt the presence of someone behind me. "Is your papa about?"

Startled, I turned and looked up into the leathery face of none other than Captain Shelby Price! I gasped, knowing I was seeing a ghost. "We thought you were—"

"Dead. Well, I was dead, but now I live. . . ."

Captain Price had changed since last I'd seen him. He was nearly bald; his bushy eyebrows, which shadowed his deep-set eyes, were peppered with gray. He appeared smaller and more frail than before. The more I looked at him standing among the cabbages and beans, the less frightening he seemed. "Sir, how could you be dead and yet still live?" I asked.

"Aye, God spared my life for a purpose," he said, anxious to tell his story. And without further invitation, and Papa nowhere to be seen, he abruptly began.

"We had been at sea for two weeks, island hopping in the Caribbean, finally coming into Mobile. I planned to round Florida and sail up the coast to Savannah and Charleston. But a day or so out of Mobile I woke one morning to a red sky. All sailors know that's a bad sign, aye 'tis."

Captain Price wiped his face with his hand, and his eyes seemed fixed on a scene only he could see. I listened carefully as the story unfolded. "By eleven bells a mighty tempest had overtaken us," he said. "But I was confident that we could ride it out, for the *Gabriel* was a good bark, and my crew was able.

"The ship rode the waves, dipping and bobbing like a big cork, then disaster hit. Lightning struck the mainmast, and it came crashing down, sweeping my pilot overboard. The ship was out of control, but before anyone could

reach the helm, a huge wave pounded us at port side. I had just enough time to grab hold to a permanent rigging rope, when the second wave hit, flipping the boat on its side. It took on water like a sieve. I remember being amazed at how fast she sank. Gone."

Captain Price's hands shook and he seemed unsteady, so I showed him to the porch, where he could sit down. I fetched him a glass of water, but hurried back so I could hear the rest of his story.

"Lost! My ship. My crew, God rest their souls," he whispered. "I clung to a plank, but there was no way for me to survive, what without food or water or a weapon to protect myself. I was a dead man; my ugly life lay in front of me like an open book. 'Lord,' I says, 'if I had it to do over, I'd do better.' Then I prepared myself to give up the ghost. Suddenly," he said, speaking just above a whisper, "a school of dolphins collected 'round—like angels they was to me. For two nights and a day those beasties kept the sharks away and nudged me along until I reached Spanish Florida. Through them God had saved my life, wretch that I am. My spirit was dead, but I live."

Captain Price finished his story. "Tell your papa that I have a new voice and I intend to use it on the side of justice, freedom, and peace." Then he left.

When Papa returned home, I told him my visitor's tale. "I think Captain Price has changed," I said, finishing. "I saw no hatefulness in his face. I heard no bitterness in his speech. You think God should forgive him?"

"It aine for me to say what God should and shouldn't do. God sees inside our hearts and knows when we have truly repented. That's what Jonah had to learn."

"Tell me what he learned, please," I asked.

As Papa tied down his tools, preparing for the coming hurricane, I took a seat on a three-legged stool and listened to the amazing story of a man who was swallowed by a big fish.

Some folk *say* one thing at the front door, then run 'round to the back door and *do* just the opposite. See, Jonah *said* he was a prophet of God. But when it came time for Jonah to actually *do* something God wanted him to do, po' Jonah fell 'way short of the mark.

God chose Jonah to do a tough chore, saying, "Go to Nineveh, Jonah—that great city of Nineveh—and tell the people they are wicked in my sight and I want them to change."

Jonah didn't want to go to Nineveh and tell the people to repent. In his mind the people of Nineveh didn't deserve an opportunity to change. No. See, Jonah figured they ought to be destroyed. So he tried to hide from God! Yes, he did. There are people who think they can go to a place where even God's eyes can't reach.

Jonah, oh foolish Jonah, slipped off to Joppa, where he boarded a ship bound for Tarshish. When he had sailed out upon the sea, a great tempest arose. The winds whirled 'round and 'round, and the ship tossed and turned on the mighty waves. The sailors grew frightened, for they knew this was no ordinary storm. Each man began to pray to his god, beggin' for deliverance. But the winds roared, and the water raged.

Meanwhile Jonah was in a deep slumber down inside the ship. The captain shook him, saying, "Wake up, sleeper. Come and speak to your God, so that perhaps this storm will not kill us all."

Jonah, oh pitiful Jonah, knew right now who had sent the storm and why. He had disobeyed God, but Jonah didn't tell anybody—no, not anybody.

When the storm still did not stop, the sailors became even more frightened. They cast lots to see who was the one who had brought such misfortune to the ship. The lot fell on Jonah. "Tell us," they asked, "who are you? Where do you come from? What have you done to bring this terror upon us?"

Jonah, oh disobedient Jonah, answered, "I am a Hebrew. The Lord God of Heaven and Earth has sent this storm 'cause I would not go to Nineveh and tell the people there to repent."

The ship tossed and turned on the mighty waves

The sailors looked from one to the other. Mountains of water rocked the ship from side to side and threatened to tip it over. "What shall we do? Oh, what shall we do?" they all cried.

Jonah, oh guilty Jonah, studied on the situation and decided there was but one thing to do. "Throw me overboard," he said. "Then the seas will calm."

But the sailors and the captain didn't want to do that. The men rowed harder and tried to steer the ship to dry land. But hard as they try, the winds blew 'gainst them.

When they saw all would be lost if they didn't act fast, the crew took hold of Jonah and cast him overboard. As soon as he hit the water he sunk like a stone, and the seas calmed. All fell peaceful-like, and the sailors knew that Jonah's God was the one true God. They sent up praises and vowed to be faithful.

Everybody thought Jonah was lost, sunk beneath the deep, dark water. But, God had other plans. Jonah was swallowed whole by a huge fish. In one big smack, he slid past the teeth, over the tongue, and down, down, down into the belly of that big fish.

Jonah, oh frightened Jonah, felt alone and helpless. Imagine the darkest place you've ever seen. And imagine the scariest place you've ever been. That's what it was like inside the belly of that fish. Jonah had no place to run or hide.

Jonah, oh prayerful Jonah, called upon the Lord, saying:

> "I called to you, God, and you answered me.
> Out of the belly of this fish I have called to you
>   and you have heard me.
> God, it was you who cast me into the deep water,
> where I thought I would never see the holy temple again.
> The water closed over my head
>   and seaweed wrapped around my head.
> I was drowning.

But you lifted me up from the pit, my God,
  for I called out to you—
Not like those who worship false gods and
  abandon them at the first sign of trouble.
I will praise you in words. Victory is the Lord's."

Jonah, oh sorrowful Jonah, talked to God for three days—prayin' mightily. Hearing Jonah's sincere pleas moved God's merciful heart. And the big fish began to swim again, up, up, up—out of the watery grave he had been buried in. Say that the fish spat Jonah out onto dry land, a little shaky, but no worse.

Sucking in a deep breath of fresh air, Jonah, oh repentant Jonah, looked up at the sun and blue skies and thanked God. He had been in darkness, but now he was in the light, and ready to do God's bidding no matter how difficult it was.

Now God said to Jonah once more and again, "Go to Nineveh and preach to the people." This time, Jonah obeyed.

The people of Nineveh changed their ways with a quickness. The anger in God's great heart was stilled and the Creator of all living things decided not to destroy Nineveh. But, Jonah, oh unforgiving Jonah, was hoppin' mad, mad enough to die.

Say, "God, I knew you were going to forgive these sinful people. I surely knew it!" he cried.

"Is it right to be so angry?" the Lord asked him.

Jonah went to a place on the east side of the city and made a shelter to sit under and pout. And there God caused a vine to grow up, and it shaded Jonah and eased his temper. But on the next day, God sent a worm to attack the plant and it died. Then a blistering east wind blew over po' Jonah's head, so hot, he wished again for death.

"Are you right to be angry 'bout the vine?" asked God.

"Yes," answered Jonah, oh sad, sad Jonah. "I am angry enough to fall out and die."

"Listen well," said God. "You're upset 'cause of a vine that you didn't plant, didn't take care of, didn't make grow. It sprang up in a night and perished in a night. Then am I not supposed to feel sorry for the thousands of people of Nineveh who don't know their right hand from their left, not to mention the po' animals?"

Even today, there're folk who think like Jonah did, who are sometimes stubborn, without compassion, and unforgiving. But God is just the opposite. No matter who we are or what we've done, if we turn from wickedness God is quick to show mercy. God's love aine fickle like ours can sometimes be. It is an eternal spring, overflowing with the sweet water of forgiveness. On this I'll say, *amen.*

By Faith

DANIEL
THE
PROPHET

The Book of Daniel

Papa was a man of simple faith. When I told him how I dreaded winter because it was always cold and damp, he'd say, "Be patient, Dumplin'. Spring is just over your shoulder." And before I knew it, one day flowers were blooming everywhere. When Mama would fret because business slowed down, Papa eased her worries with a loving pat on the hand. "Be strong. Live by faith. It will get better." And it always did.

Where had he learned to be so sure about himself and God? Whenever I asked Papa, he always gave credit to the Reverend Silas Jefferies, without adding any of the details I longed to hear. Papa could talk to a crowd about Moses, Queen Esther, and Jonah, but he got tongue-tied when he tried to talk about *his* past. I wanted to know more about my father and his special friendship with the Reverend Jefferies.

I'd never met Papa's mentor, but Mama said he was a freeman of color who'd earned his freedom fighting in the Revolutionary War, and that he had been a founding member of the Brown Fellowship Society. "No finer man lived in Charleston," she'd said. Papa had admired the Reverend Jefferies so much, he'd changed his name to Jefferies to honor him.

Then one winter day, Papa took me to the Brown Fellowship Society's Cemetery, where the reverend was buried. Usually Papa visited his old friend alone. I figured taking me along was his way of saying that part of his life was open to discussion. And I had lots and lots of questions.

Tracing the letter "J" on the headstone, I asked gently, "When did you meet the Reverend Jefferies?"

Papa pulled a few dead vines from the grave. "Strange how people come into yo' life. As a sapling back in Africa, I was picked to be the apprentice of a great Mende blacksmith. I was proud, and lorded over the other boys, saying I was chosen 'cause I was smarter'n them. Then I was caught and sold to

Captain Price, and all that young pride was crushed 'neath the heel of slavery. Years later, after I'd bought my freedom, I daresome to dream again— maybe of being a blacksmith. I commenced to lookin' 'round for a way to make that happen. Now, ever-body—blacks and whites—say the Reverend Jefferies was Charleston's best blacksmith, and I wanted to learn from the best. So, I visited him at his forge. He listened to my story and took me on as his apprentice."

"I never knew that," I said.

Papa stood thoughtfully by the grave for a few minutes. He reached out and touched the marble headstone, then he turned and walked away.

"You still miss him, don't you?" I said tentatively.

"The Reverend Jefferies stood as my father, my brother, my teacher, my best friend, and yes, I still miss him," he answered. "From Monday through Saturday, he and me worked side by side, and at night he taught me to read and write and figure numbers. On Sundays a few of us gathered on his porch or sat by his fireplace to hear stories of faith, hope, courage, and love—the same stories I now tell you."

When we turned down Meeting Street the heavens opened, and it poured down, a cold, penetrating rain. Papa and I stepped inside a doorway until it slackened. He told me then that the Reverend Jefferies' forge had been located on Tradd Street. After the Reverend Jefferies had died, it was run by his son-in-law, Raymond Thomas. But after a few years it had gone out of business.

"Why didn't you stay on and work with Mr. Thomas?" I asked, curious to know why Papa'd chosen to open his shop on East Battery.

Papa's face darkened with the question. "Raymond had been after the Reverend Jefferies to buy slaves so's to cut expenses," he explained. "But the Reverend Jefferies would have rather shut down than use slave labor. When

Raymond took charge, the first thing he did was buy two boys, 'specting me to train them. When I wouldn't, he threw me out, saying I wasn't a good blacksmith."

"Who would believe that?" I shouted in disbelief.

Papa went on. "I had used all my savings to buy Mama's freedom, so I didn't have 'nough money to start my own business. I had lost my best friend, my job—everything, even my hope. I got scared; even considered givin' up my freedom and going back to sea."

I put my hand in his, and he squeezed it gently. Though I wanted to know more, he looked so sad, I didn't push him to continue. By then, the rain had slowed to a dreary, January drizzle. We hurried on our way.

But once we reached home, and our feet were warming by the fire, Papa took up the conversation where he'd left off. "I'd 'bout made up my mind to head back out to sea. As I opened my sea chest to pack it, to my everlasting surprise there was a note and a few gold pieces inside, put there by the Reverend Jefferies before he died. The money helped, but the note did more. That li'l piece of paper gave me the strength to stay in Charleston—and to hang out my own blacksmith's sign."

"How could just a note do all that?" I asked.

"The words the Reverend Jefferies wrote were few, but powerful. They showed me how to stop doubting myself, and to trust God. That note helped me find my faith."

"What did it say?"

Papa knew the words by heart: " 'When the lions of life surround you, remember Daniel.' "

"Why Daniel?" I wanted to know.

Papa was smiling lovingly at me now, and suddenly I felt closer to him than at any time I could remember. Outside, it was cold and wet, but I felt warm and secure. And as we sipped Mama's root tea, Papa began the story of Daniel, a lone man who faced a den full of lions.

Like Samuel, and Jonah, Daniel was a prophet of God, a good and just man, who loved the Lord with all his mind, with all his heart, and with all his soul. And God never failed him. No.

Daniel b'longed to the royal house of Judah. But when he was a young man, he was captured and took from Jerusalem to Babylon where he grew up in King Nebuchadnezzar's court. There he found all kinds of gods for people to worship. Some had the body of a man and the head of a bull. Some had the wings of eagles, and others were made of wood, iron, and stone. But Daniel was steadfast in his love for the one God.

They tell me Daniel's loyalty won him much praise. He was even noticed by ol' King Nebuchadnezzar hisself, who gave him a high position in his government—put Daniel over all the wise men of Babylon. Yes he did.

Daniel did such a good job, he soon was the envy of lesser men. They tried all manner of trickery to get Daniel to fall out of favor with King Nebuchadnezzar. But Daniel was loved by many others, and these schemes and plots failed.

Came to pass, King Nebuchadnezzar died, and Darius became king. He, too, liked what he saw in Daniel and gave him a position of power. Darius organized his kingdom by putting one hundred and twenty princes over all the land. Then he placed three presidents over the princes. Daniel was one of the presidents.

Sad to say, the princes and presidents 'llowed themselves to be overtook by jealousy toward po' Daniel. Oh, it fell on them like a night fever and made them hot with anger. Like spiders in a bottle, they wove a wicked web in which to ensnare him, all on account of Daniel trying to do right.

First, they tried to make others believe Daniel was a foreigner who had betrayed the king's trust, by cheatin' and stealin' money—but Daniel was found innocent of all charges. Well then, they tried to tear down Daniel's good name—but couldn't find a thing to tarnish his character. Next, these princes and presidents tried to prove that Daniel was not faithful to the king—but even there he was found to be without fault. At last, when the princes and presidents had no more fingers to point, they decided to use Daniel's own faith against him.

Hear me now, this is what they did. The princes and presidents tricked Darius into signing an order that prayers and petitions to any God had to be made to Darius. Anybody caught disobeying this order was sent to death in the lions' den.

When Daniel heard 'bout the new law, he went right on praying three times a day, same as always. He had nothing to hide, nothing to deny. He even left his window open for all to hear and see. That is just what the princes and presidents had hoped for. They took that bone and ran straight to the king with it.

"Lord Darius, listen. Daniel is prayin'. We've seen him with our own eyes. We've heard him with our own ears. And according to the law *you* signed, he's got to be put to death in the lions' den."

Say King Darius was sick at heart 'cause he'd been tricked. He didn't want to kill that good man, no, no. But with nothing else to do, he ordered Daniel to be put in the den with the big, hungry lions.

"The God you love and serve will deliver you," the king called out to him as he put his seal on the stone that covered the mouth of the den. Then he turned sadly and returned to the royal palace to wait until the next morning.

All through the night, King Darius walked back and forth, unable to eat or sleep. His soul was heavy, and his mind deeply troubled. Would that long night ever end?

At first light, Darius come rushing to the lions' den calling Daniel. "Did yo' God protect you as I have hoped?" And thanks be to the living God, Daniel answered back! "I am well. My Lord sent an angel to shut the lions' mouths, and they were unable to hurt me."

Before their wondering eyes the stone was removed, and Daniel walked out whole, untouched.

Daniel walked out whole, untouched

When King Darius saw that his friend was safe, he turned his anger toward the wicked princes and presidents and he punished them without mercy. Now they and their families where thrown in the lions' den.

Then the king wrote out another law, which decreed that throughout the land his people were to worship the God of Daniel, the One True God. Daniel was restored to his high place in the government, where he served Darius and later Cyrus the Persian, who succeeded him.

In the first year of his reign, Cyrus allowed the captive Jews to return to their homeland and rebuild the temple in Jerusalem. Oh what a rejoicing there was among the people of Queen Esther and Daniel, for they had been in captivity for over seventy years. At last, they were free once more and again.

Now when the snarling lions of life surround you, remember Daniel. Cling to your faith; have no doubts. God's promises of salvation are true.

Chain of Faith, Hope, and Love

THE BOOK
OF PROVERBS

In 1816, two weeks after my sixteenth birthday, I was invited by Jerena Lee, a leader in the newly formed African Methodist Episcopal Church, to come help teach young children in Philadelphia about personal grooming, health, and hygiene. I was anxious to go.

When I asked Papa, he hesitated, saying, "I'm not ready to turn my daughter loose in the world like something wild." But after Mama spoke to him, he finally gave his slow permission. He knew that once I left, it wouldn't be safe for me to come back home.

The night before I sailed, Mama and Papa invited families from the Brown Fellowship Society to say good-bye. All the people I cared about came to wish me well. We feasted on boiled chicken and rice, stewed tomatoes, fresh shell beans, spoon bread, and for dessert, molasses shortcake.

When we'd finished, Mama presented me with a beautiful whalebone hair comb she and Papa had bought from a seaman. "Remember us with love when you wear it," she said.

Mr. Riz Greene, a family friend, stood and raised his hands to get our attention. "Our Mis Charlotte is fixin' to sojourn in a strange land," he said. "So I want to give her this li'l saying to remember: 'Wisdom builds the house,'" he said. "'Good judgment makes it secure; knowledge furnishes the rooms with all kinds of grand things.'"

When the last banjo note floated away on the night wind, and the laughter of my friends died down, I sat with Papa on the porch. "I liked the saying Mr. Greene recited," I told him. "Where did it come from?"

"Comes from Proverbs 24: 3–4," Papa answered, leaning back against the wall of the house.

"I've always found Proverbs a little hard to understand," I said.

Papa nodded, saying, "You have to study on Proverbs, look inside the words for their deeper meaning. Think of them as a golden chain, the links of which are formed by faith, hope, and love. Always keep in mind that this is not a chain that binds, but a lifeline to hold on to as you make your way through this ol' troubled world."

"Do you have a favorite?"

"Here's a Proverb to begin your journey," he answered.

> "Take good care of your heart better than
>   some worldly thing,
> 'cause the heart is the source of life.
> Watch your mouth—don't lie or speak cruelly to others.
> Look ahead, never backward,
> but keep your eyes fixed
>   on the path where your feet are
>   taking you, and you'll be safe.
> Go neither to the right nor the left,
>   and above all, keep away from all manner of evil."

Then Papa handed me his Bible, the one the Reverend Jefferies had given him. I tried to refuse it because I knew how much this Bible meant to him. But he put the well-worn book in my hands firmly. "When times are good, read it for joy. When times are hard, read it for comfort. When you are confused, read it for guidance. When you are lonely, read it for pleasure and the sheer beauty of the words. But most of all, try not to let it collect dust," he said, chuckling softly.

There was so much I wanted to say to Papa, but nothing seemed enough. I pressed his Bible to my heart, saying, "Thank you for everything."

As I waved good-bye the next morning, I felt sad that this chapter of my life—with Papa, Mama, and all the people I knew—had come to a close, but I was excited about what was ahead. Whatever awaited me, I felt hopeful, prepared—ready for the challenge.

The introductory prayer comes from *Conversations with God: Two Centuries of Prayers by African-Americans*, edited by James Melvin Washington, PhD.

Charlotte's Introduction

In 1860 the population of the United States was 31,433,790 people. American blacks numbered about 4.5 million, and of those blacks, half a million were free. Approximately half of the free blacks of 1860 lived in slave states.

Something Wonderful Out of Nothing — *The Creation*

After the 1800 slave rebellion organized by Gabriel Prosser failed in Richmond, Virginia, slaveholders all over the South feared other rebellions might take place unless they took measures to stop them. States began passing restrictive laws that limited the movement of both slaves and free blacks. In Charleston free blacks were required to have in their possession proof of their free status or risk being kidnapped and re-enslaved.

We have intentionally avoided using any gender pronouns for God, and have instead used all the traditional and some nontraditional names—Lord included.

We used the Genesis 1:27 version of the creation of humankind.

Making Choices — *The Fall* and *Cain and Abel*

In March 1807, Congress banned the trans-Atlantic slave trade, prohibiting "the importation of slaves into the United States or the territories thereof," effective January 1, 1808. The illegal importation of slaves continued up until the end of the Civil War. The last shipment of slaves entered the United States at Mobile Bay, Alabama, in 1859 onboard the *Clothilde.*

Free blacks could buy and/or inherit slaves. When President Abraham Lincoln signed the Emancipation Proclamation, ninety-one free blacks living in Charleston owned 268 slaves.

A Love Worth Waiting For — *Jacob and Rachel*

During the first two decades of the nineteenth century, Charleston slaveowners often freed their personal slaves, permitted them to buy their own freedom, or allowed free blacks to buy their family members. To keep this from happening too often, the state of South Carolina passed a law requiring the approval of the state House of Representatives before a slave could be freed.

The average cost of a female domestic slave in 1800 was approximately $100, but prices ranged from as low as $50 for a motherless infant to $500 for a skilled craftsman.

It is important to note that Abraham is the patriarch of three religions: Judaism, Christianity, and Islam.

How Can You Forgive? — *The Story of Joseph*

In 1800, it was not against the law in Virginia or South Carolina to teach a slave how to read or write. Many slaves were quite literate, fluent in several languages, and often carried on the master's financial business with integrity. However, after several literate slaves led rebellions, slave states from New York to Georgia began passing rigid laws forbidding slaves an education. Most masters immediately sold a slave who could read and write, believing him or her to be a threat to his authority.

Your God Is My God — *Ruth and Naomi*

When slaves got too old or too sick to be of benefit to their masters, it was common practice to free them. Sick and unable to care for themselves, many of these people died. But some of them went on to live useful lives in freedom, much to the dismay of their masters.

Basket-making is a time-honored tradition in South Carolina. The coiled baskets made from the Carolina sweetgrass were sought-after household items as well as beautiful expressions of art. This coiled technique, still used in South Carolina, can be traced to West African roots.

Freed slaves who left the South rarely returned. Fearful of the importation of rebel influences, Southern slaveowners passed laws forbidding blacks to re-enter the state once they were freed. They returned at the risk of being captured and resold.

To Slay a Giant — *David and Goliath*

Peter Willy's story is based on Henry "Box" Brown, who was shipped from Richmond to Philadelphia by the Adams Express Company.

We have included the Psalms in this story, even though David had not written the Psalms when he faced Goliath. We feel the language and ideas expressed in some of the Psalms were a part of David's thoughts even when he was a young boy.

No Greater Love — *Queen Esther*

The "Dungeon," a place where slaves were held before sale, was an actual place in Charleston. Mis Moreau, a fictional character, represents that unknown quantity of mulatto men and women who lived as whites. By law a person with any black ancestor, no matter how distant, was considered black and subject to unjust laws and codes. Since there was no way to tell a fair-skinned black from a white, some legally black people "passed." Some of them, such as Ellen Craft, who escaped slavery by passing as her husband's master, became abolitionists, while others led quiet and private lives.

A Change of Heart—*The Story of Jonah*

Sailors brought the weather and other news. Because of their mobility upon the seas, free black sailors played an important role in the abolitionist movement. In the early 1800s they kept the black community informed about the Haitian revolution, maroon activities on the Caribbean islands, and successful revolts and uprisings in Mexico, Brazil, and other South American slaveholding countries. Following a series of attempted revolts in South Carolina, New York, and Virginia, Charleston began passing a series of laws requiring black sailors to submit to imprisonment while their ships were in port.

There are documented stories, dating back to ancient times, of dolphins saving the lives of sailors.

By Faith — *Daniel the Prophet*

The street names are from a map of Charleston, circa 1820.

The title "Reverend" was often bestowed upon a person who was especially devout.

Some slaves were freed after serving honorably in the Revolutionary War.

There was no African American church congregation in Charleston before 1817. The first church in Charleston was Hampstead African Methodist Episcopal Church, established by Morris Brown. Denmark Vesey was a devout member. Richard Allen, the founder of the Free African Society, was a minister in the church, and its first bishop.

According to Patrick R. McNaughton in *The Mande Blacksmiths*, blacksmiths were both glorified and feared within the Mande culture. Anthropologist Laura Makarius has described the conflicting status of the blacksmith:

By a strange paradox, this noted craftsman, whose bold and meritorious services are indispensable to his community, had been relegated to a position outside the place of society, almost as an "untouchable." Regarded as a possessor of great magical powers, held at the same time in veneration and contempt, entrusted with duties unrelated to his craft or to his inferior social status . . . his figure presents . . . a mass of contradictions. (McNaughton, p. xiii) This is the tradition to which Price would have been introduced before he was captured at age ten.

For the Opening Stories

Appiah, Kwame Anthony. *In My Father's House: African Philosophy of Culture.* New York: Oxford University Press, 1992.

DeVorsey, Louis, Jr., and Marion J. Rice. *The Plantation South: Atlanta to Savannah and Charleston.* New Brunswick, NJ: Rutgers University Press, 1992.

Freedman, Samuel G. *Upon This Rock: The Miracles of a Black Church.* New York: HarperCollins, 1993.

Genovese, Eugene D. *Roll, Jordan, Roll.* New York: Vintage Books, 1974.

Joyner, Charles. *Down by the Riverside: A South Carolina Slave Community.* Urbana and Chicago: University of Illinois Press, 1985.
————. *Remember Me: Slave Life in Coastal Georgia.* Atlanta: Georgia Humanities Council, 1989.

Kroger, Larry. *Black Slave Owners: Free Black Slave Masters in South Carolina, 1790–1860.* Columbia: University of South Carolina Press, 1995.

McNaughton, Patrick R. *The Mande Blacksmiths.* Bloomington and Indianapolis: University of Indiana Press, 1993.

McNerney, Kathryn. *Antique Iron Identification and Values.* Paducah, KY: Collector Books, 1991.

Raboteau, Albert J. *A Fire in the Bones: Reflections on African-American Religious History.* Boston: Beacon Press, 1995.
———— *Slave Religion: The "Invisible Institution" in the Antebellum South.* New York: Oxford University Press, 1980.

Vernon, Amelia Wallace. *African Americans at Mars Bluff, South Carolina.* Columbia: University of South Carolina Press, 1993.

Vlach, John Michael. *Charleston Blacksmith: The Work of Philip Simmons* (Rev. ed.). Columbia: University of South Carolina Press, 1992.

Washington, James Melvin, PhD. *Conversations with God: Two Centuries of Prayers by African-Americans.* New York: HarperCollins, 1994.

For the Bible Stories

Hartman, Louis F. *Encyclopedic Dictionary of the Bible.* New York: McGraw-Hill, 1963.

Henry, Matthew. *Commentary on the Whole Bible—Genesis to Revelation.* Tulsa: Port City Bible Company, 1972.

The King James Version of the Bible

The New English Bible: The Old Testament. Oxford, England: Oxford University Press and Cambridge University Press, 1970.

Unger, Merrill F. *Unger's Bible Dictionary.* Chicago: Moody Press, 1982.

Wood, Peter H. *Black Majority: Negroes in Colonial South Carolina from 1670 through the Stono Rebellion.* New York: W. W. Norton and Company, reissued 1996.